A Daughter'

A Daughter's Legacy

Pamphilia Hlapa

UNIVERSITY OF KwaZulu-Natal Press

Published in 2006 by University of KwaZulu-Natal Press
Private Bag X01, Scottsville, 3209
South Africa
Email: books@ukzn.ac.za
Website: www.ukznpress.co.za

ISBN 1-86914-085-0

Editor: Andrea Nattrass
Cover designer: Sebastien Quevauvilliers, Flying Ant Designs
Typesetter: RockBottom Design

Printed and bound by Interpak Books, Pietermaritzburg

Author's Note

I know Kedibone's story. I have seen my friends, my cousins, my sister and my mother endure her pain in silence. Kedibone did not suffer alone. She represents the stories of the boy-children and girl-children whom society and culture have failed.

As she nurtures her child, Kedibone wonders, what if her insecurities, her hurt and her pain, her fear and her anger damage her son in a way that she cannot handle? Will her son forgive her for that?

These are questions that many women, myself included, ask themselves today in their role as mothers. They look back to those days when they were unable to perceive the implications of the perpetual and universal victimisation of slaughtered beginnings, of cultural expectations and taboos, of broken societal promises and values, of mothers' and fathers' failure to raise mothers and fathers, and of society's lack of competence in raising healthy men and women who can parent their own children.

But there comes a time in your life when you finally get it. In the midst of everything, you stop and say 'enough crying and struggling to hold on'. When you do that, a sense of serenity is born of your acceptance; a new-found confidence is born of self-approval. You stop blaming yourself and other people for things they did to you or did not do for you. You acquire a new sense of safety and security from self-reliance when you learn to stand on your own. As Ralph Waldo Emerson said: 'Whoso would be a [person] must be a nonconformist. Nothing is at last sacred but the integrity of your own mind.' A sense of peace and contentment is born from forgiveness. You forgive yourself and others and you move on with your new life.

When I think about this book, I think of the girls and women in the community that I come from, the pains they suffer and the struggles they face each day in order to defend and uphold our cultural beliefs and secrets. Everything is always about what is socially and culturally acceptable, what you can talk about and what you cannot talk about. You can die as long as you die within cultural confinements; only then is your death dignified. It is in honour of these girls and women that I have written this book.

I know that in this part of the world, reading is not part of the culture. Even more importantly, the girls and women in my home community will not have the money to buy this book. Moreover, they will not fully understand the language in which this book is written. But my courage and strength to live on and tell the truth will inspire them. It will reach out to them and they will know that there is hope in this life. We share the same struggles and pain that we have shared for a long time; all of us suffer silently and individually with the fear of disturbing the normal day-to-day activities of the community.

We walked through the same dust; we went to the same schools; we all watched in horror when crimes of rape were committed against all of us, our family members and our friends. We watched the traumatic deaths of young girls due to backstreet abortions. We watched the horrors of single motherhood consume the lives of teenagers. We watched some of our friends and families die of HIV/Aids; people dying without purpose. And as for those who survived, we watched them die inside as they lost hope.

People carry on with life without realising the power within themselves to enjoy the greatness of life and the freedom to make choices. I watched mothers lose hope in their children's lives and the future. I cry every time I go back there because the girls I know and grew up with are not the same girls any more. They are consumed by pain and fears, cultural taboos and pressures to surrender to mediocrity. Some have become wives at an early age; some got sold into marriages in order to escape poverty and the fear of facing the world alone. They were forced to surrender their personal power and will to live to the pressures of their world because there is no other life they know.

Throughout the writing of this book, I have remembered Dalia, Tebogo, Angela, Mmabatho, Mosibudi, Khomotso and Winnifred. In that very same dusty village, lie my roots – the roots that I will honour and cherish all the days of my life, the roots that taught me survival and resilience. They taught me respect and tolerance for my fellow human beings and the value of faith and prayer. I honour those roots and the lives of my friends who died before they could find courage, as well as those who have suffered the hardships of poverty and the cruelty of child molestation, rape and sexual abuse. It is my prayer that one day this book will be translated into the language they will all understand, the language they can identify with, so that they can find some comfort and hope in the story.

I know they still hold the belief that it is culturally wrong to reveal certain things that are considered taboo. It is culturally wrong for a woman to reach the age of 21 without a child. It does not matter whether you are married or not; you have to have a child to prove you are not barren. Children are born out of children; they become an extension of the family and they grow up knowing their mothers as their older sisters. It is culturally acceptable to end up in a career you do not even like because all that matters is that you put food on the table. It is also acceptable to be sick and to die of poverty-induced illnesses and diseases. Malnutrition and poor health conditions will merit sympathetic support. Mental illnesses and psychological disorders are seen as either the results of witchcraft or as a punishment from the angry ancestors.

It is acceptable for a woman to stay and suffer in an unhealthy marriage because culturally *lebitla la mosadi ke bogadi*, meaning 'a woman's death and grave is in her marriage'. Once you get married, it is expected that you should stay there no matter what you endure. You should never go back home because you will shame your family. You just need to 'hold on' until you die.

Your own brother can sleep with your wife while you are at work and everybody in the village will know about it except you. Boys and men can force women into sex and never take responsibility for the support of the children born out of those relations. Your family will tell you to 'leave him alone, this child is ours and we will not fail to support it'. But nobody at home earns a decent salary.

What kinds of mothers and fathers are we nurturing for our future descendants? Boys do not know how to grow up and become real fathers. They ill-treat women and they know they can get away with it.

You are taught not to question but to abide and listen to your elders in the name of respect. If you challenge anything, the thinking goes, you will end up having a lot of bad luck and mishaps in your life and you will be miserable until you die. When you grow up, everything is about survival. From an early age you start believing that you do not have a choice. In most cases, you are expected to give in to the pressures. If you fight, you are viewed as a rebel. This will not earn you any moral support at all because you will be seen as bringing scandal to the community.

I did not question. I did not ask. I did not talk. But I still suffered and became miserable. Please do not get me wrong. I am not attacking my culture in terms of its identity, roots and ancestral heritage. The true meaning and strength of my culture is very evident in all aspects of my life and I am proud of that.

Now, however, I question the culture of ignorance, of encouraging irresponsible behaviour, of embracing poverty, embracing fears and pain, of self-doubt, a culture of laziness, silence and unhealthy habits.

In my culture people are not ashamed to say, '*ditsela tsa monna ga di botsiswe*' ('you do not question a man's behaviour'). It is culturally disrespectful to challenge things such as this. Some parents are even proud that their sons have inherited adulterous behaviour and nothing can be done about it. They say, 'No, he is born into a family of cheaters, so he cannot run away from it.'

While I am against all these things, I remain very proud of my roots and my cultural identity. I am proud to say that our roots are very strong and if we take that strength with us, no battle will be a losing one. However, the slow pace at which things move can hold people back, can prevent them from recognising the true value of their roots and from realising that there is always another chance to improve things in their lives.

People embrace those vicious circles in the name of heritage because they get support from the community. Everybody is asking, 'Why me? Why do these things keep happening to me? I must be weak.' They see their background and childhood as a weakness rather than an enriching experience. Hence they never want to talk about it.

I decided to lead a new life. I do not want to be fragile, weak and vulnerable any more. One important reality for me is that even in silence, when you are alone with your thoughts, you know that the pain and fear are a part of you. Do you deny the realities of your past or do you condemn them? In silence, you may try to fight those realities. Some drink them away, some work them away, some romance them away, and some kill themselves and die with them. Some people tell themselves those realities do not get in their way. I have learned the hard way that this is a lie I now refuse to believe.

Well, I am talking now and perhaps because of everything I have to say, my ancestors are tossing and turning in their graves over my delinquency and because I broke the silence. Because I have become a rabble-rouser, fate-tempting or not, my children will not be subjected to any of those constraints and I will teach them to make choices. My children are not going to live life through my eyes and those of my community.

To my son and my mother.

When I started writing this book, my only sister was still alive and I wish she had lived to see it published. This book is also dedicated to the memory of my late sister Daphney Ephodia Mokgadi.

Between my sister and my mother, I learned how to be a woman. I will never forget how my sister used to shout loudly from the house while I was hanging the washing outside, 'Bright colours first!' When she died, the colours of my washing got even brighter but, this time, the dark ones needed to be hung first.

And now, to the memory of my departed son Ebrahim Rorisang who was stillborn. Heaven only knows why to date I have only conceived boys.

1

'Rain, rain, go away; come again another day; little Kedibone wants to play; rain, rain go away.'

Being the youngest child seemed like a great good fortune to me. I loved singing this song while hopping around our veranda. It was my way of showing excitement. I was only four years old and loved by everyone – the apple of my parents' eyes. I was not yet aware of the world around me, but if I had been, I would have been confident it owed me safety and protection. I believed my parents were there to look after me.

The area I grew up in was an underdeveloped and poor one. The women relied on their fields to grow mealies and other vegetables. Those who were lucky had husbands who worked in Johannesburg. My father was one of those men. He was away from home for long periods, only returning on a handful of occasions a year – at month ends, Christmas, and for other seasonal festivities. December was always the longest time that he was home.

I received all the attention I needed from everyone around me. During the day, because there were no day-care or crèche facilities available, I would go to school with my mother who was a schoolteacher. I was allowed the privilege of sitting in her classroom while she gave lessons. Even though I was still too young to be registered at the school I managed to absorb some of the teachings. 'Kedibone is mommy's little angel in the blue train,' my mother would say with pride to her colleagues. They knew how expensive and wonderful the South African blue train was. I knew that when my mother said this she was proud of me.

I was an outgoing, free-spirited little girl, although I was once terrified of a white man who was in our yard to drill a borehole for the water pump. The whole day, I hid behind the door to make sure the white man never found me, amusing everyone at home with my actions. It was probably because our village was about sixty kilometres away from the city. We never went to town unless we were taken to the hospital to see Dr Omar, who was Indian. To all of us children in the village, a white man was a complete stranger who terrified us.

I also had a very strong fear of ghosts. I often told my mother that I had seen a ghost in the house next door, which had been abandoned when the parents died. I would tell my mother that I saw a tall male ghost, 'A fala pitsa ya maoto ka mo morago ga ntlo', meaning 'the ghost was cleaning the four-legged pot that was used on the outside fire behind the house'.

I had no other worries because my daddy was still alive. When he came home for the holidays, I would have the best times with him. Though he was a very quiet man, he made our times together enjoyable. He made the finest angel delight puddings, which he learned from his job in Johannesburg. I would sit on his lap while reciting our family praise song with pride, and daddy would give me a hug and a kiss. Sometimes he even used to tape-record me when I was singing.

One day in 1979, I saw everyone running to their homes, with big trucks full of soldiers and dogs chasing them. During the night, my mother and all the older people packed our household belongings and loaded all of them into trucks. This was called mokhudugo, meaning 'forced relocation to another land by the government'. An area had been prepared for the entire community in another village about two hours' drive from where we were, but my mother decided we would not go to that village. Instead, we would go to my maternal grandmother's village, which was in the same vicinity though under a different chief.

When we arrived, we moved into my mother's uncle's house, which was large and white and had many rooms. It was different from my paternal grandmother's home, which consisted of a four-cornered house with a corrugated iron roof and one thatched rondavel house. My excitement was mixed with confusion and a lack of knowledge as to what was happening to us. My mother was not going to be staying with us because she could not get a teaching post in the village.

I was left with my siblings – two brothers and one sister – along with our cousins who lived in the house. I had to learn to get on with them and to make new friends. I was now separated from my father's relatives, but at least I was close to my maternal grandmother. Our new house was being built and it was going to be big as well.

My eldest brother, Matome, had to look after us with the help of our nearby relatives who would come in now and again to check on us. Matome had to learn how to be a brother, a mother and a father. He would take my youngest brother, Sipho, along with the cousins to the river to catch fish for supper. At night they would sit in a small hut built with *mahlaka* (the remains of the mealie crops after harvesting) while waiting to trap birds so that we could have something to eat with our morning porridge.

We were all registered in the schools around the village. Sipho and I went to the same school inside the village and Matome and my sister Angela went to the farm school outside the village.

Although I was only five years old, I was accepted at the local lower primary school, mainly because my mother was a teacher and she was very well known and well connected. Being a teacher carried a great deal of status in the community and our mother's colleagues treated us like royalty. In winter, on our way to school, Sipho and I would stop at our grandmother's house where she would give us burnt stones wrapped in brown paper so that we could warm up our tiny hands and not feel the cold.

There was a shortage of classrooms and so the schedules for lessons were divided into two groups: a morning group and an afternoon group. The pupils alternated groups. If you attended morning class one day, you would be with the afternoon group the following day. I loved staying on at school even if I had attended the morning class. It did not matter to me because I knew I could walk back home at any time as long as it was still light. The journey would involve stopping at the homes of my new friends, Dalia, Mmabatho and Dikeledi. I also knew that my maternal grandmother's house was on the way home. I would play with my cousins and they could walk me home if it got late.

What I loved about stopping at granny's house was that all of us would share a meal in one big plate and bowl. During harvesting times, granny would cook mealies, *ditloo, dinyebu, maraka* and *marotse*. She would prepare us *thopi* (porridge made with only pumpkin) and we enjoyed other home-grown vegetables and fruits. Koko (granny) as all the grandparents were called, would also give us *letsweleba* (soft porridge cooked in the process of preparing home-brewed beer). The people in the village enjoyed drinking the beer together and would also brew a drink from the marula fruit. It was a social and community obligation always to ensure there was beer for the weekend. People would flock to the house with the beer and drink and would make too much noise. We would play our games outside in the yards and there was no fear of being knocked down by a car because there were few of those.

'*Piki, piki, mabelane, sala, sala gentleman, aka matwo, thika le lotia, pulana, pulana so tila. Makakabele s, s, s, s, phuma wena, sala wena.*' This was one of the songs I sang with my friends as we

4

played endless games of hide-and-seek. There were plenty of other activities and new games, and I enjoyed waiting in the small huts with my brothers while they trapped birds. I was still scared of ghosts. This time I was scared of my grandfather's ghost because I had heard he died before I was born and there was a big photograph of him in my grandmother's house. I thought he would come down and scare me. My fear of ghosts was real and everybody sympathised with me, except for Sipho, who teased me about it.

Sipho is five years older than I am and we never saw eye to eye. We always fought and he would take advantage of my small size and the fact that I was a girl. He would beat me up and make sure I did not tell anyone by threatening me and reminding me that our mother did not like it if we lied. Because of my status as the youngest, my mother feared I would be too spoilt and would turn into a brat if she defended me from my brother. She would never entertain our fights, which were mostly motivated by sibling rivalry. Sipho did not like the fact that he was supposed to be the last child, and then I had come along.

While we played our games, adults carried on with their day-to-day activities – eking out a living and enjoying small things such as drinking home-brewed beer. Poverty was part of us.

2

I continued to attend extra afternoon classes until one day on my way back from school something happened that as an adult I believe destroyed my spark and the excitement in my eyes for good. The memory is still fresh in my mind even today. I was six years old and was walking home alone from school. I had my school bag hanging on my shoulder and had only walked a few metres away from the school yard to the white house with a treed fence on the corner. A guy whose face I remember forced himself on top of me around the corner where you could hide behind the fence. I had no idea what he was doing to me. All I can recall is being unable to scream; my face and head were hurting due to the pressure he was putting on my neck. Except for telling me he would cut my throat if I screamed he did not say anything to me. He held a small knife in his hand while he forcefully pulled down my underwear and unzipped his trousers to pull out his 'thing'. I was so young I had no idea what he was doing to me except that he was hurting me. Before I knew it my tiny body was on the ground with my legs apart and his 'thing' being forced inside my private parts. I was trembling in shock, pain and agony and my voice was stuck inside me. I waited for him to finish what he was doing. I can't even close my eyes now without seeing his image.

He did what he wanted to do and once he was done, he stood up and I did not even want to see what he was doing. I think I lay still for a while, wondering if he was completely done and what was supposed to happen next. I tried to cry out but I was so lame with pain and fear that my voice could not come out. I can picture my face, so red and my eyes swollen. I touched my private parts to feel what was happening. I was bleeding and there was pain and fluids. I realised my panties were torn on the side but I pulled them up. I only wanted to cover myself and stand up to walk home. When I stood up, I realised I was all alone and I could not walk properly because of all the pressure in my genitals and the pain in my body. Even though I did not know what the guy had done, I felt invaded and shocked. I slowly picked up my school bag, which I had been lying on all along. My school dress was full of soil and it had creased but I did not care. I knew that people would think I had been playing after school, and it was normal for me to arrive home with dirty clothes.

I had no idea how to explain what had happened to me. I was also convinced I had been punished for attending the afternoon class when I knew I did not have anyone to walk back home with me. I had never heard anyone talk about sex before, let alone rape or child molestation. I had no idea of the purpose of my private parts other than answering the call of nature. The worst was that my mother was working away from home and we were left in the care of nannies; no one noticed anything or bothered to ask me anything. When I got home I was still crying but I later realised I had to keep quiet – I had no idea what to say or to whom or why. I remember that for the rest of the week, I told my teachers that I had terrible headaches each time they saw me cry. They thought I did not want to be at school and on the second day, my teacher sent me home. From that day onwards, I started seeing fluids on my underwear, but I still did not say anything to anyone. Even when my mother came home, she did not notice anything and life went on around me.

But things had changed for me. I could no longer accept defeat while playing *kgati* (a rope-skipping game) and *diketo* (a game played with small stones in a round hole designed to teach children how to count) with the other children. I became aggressive and wanted to play only if the other children would let me start the game. Being the one to start was very important – you got to compete as the first player and it increased your chances of winning. Most of the games were very competitive ones where there had to be a winner, and suddenly winning was important to me. My carefree spirit was dead and I would throw tantrums if I lost a game. I wanted attention.

My ongoing aggression became so bad that during her weekend visits, my mother started thinking I was becoming a brat. She tried to discipline me but the harder she tried the more aggressive and stubborn I became with other children and my brother Sipho. I started to enjoy bullying my friends when playing with them. I always wanted them to make me a winner. I was very emotional and manipulative but my desire to win made me a very determined pupil at school. I was also under some pressure to perform well as I was a teacher's daughter – I had no other option. When I failed to perform I would make myself sick and the teachers would send me home early.

We moved into our new house at the beginning of the new year. Matome went to stay with relatives in another village. My mother found a position at my school and came back home. One of our cousins, Moyahabo, came to stay with us and I fought with her a lot. The new house was beautiful and big and my mother worked hard to create a home for us. Our family was one of the privileged few because both our parents were working.

With my mother's return, I had to change my behaviour. I had to be a good girl or else I would receive one of my mother's hidings that I feared very much. I became a clown – entertaining people, telling jokes and being the centre of attraction. I loved

9

the attention I created for myself. It helped to distract me because I started playing *kgati* and *diketo* again.

I became very sickly. My head was covered with *dipudi* (ringworm). I had to have my head shaved and I wore a white bandage all the time, only removing it on the days I was taken to the clinic to get it dressed and the *dipudi* cleaned up so that it did not become septic. Koko Mokgokoloshi would come every third day to shave my head with a razor blade so that my hair did not grow back and get stuck to the bandage, which would then make it difficult to remove. When the *dipudi* was gone, I had *sehahahane* (chicken pox) and *mauwe* (measles) and my granny had to look after me while my mother was at work. She would pick me up in the morning and drop me off later in the afternoon.

'*Re fihlile, re fihlile naa?*' ('Are we there, are we there yet?')

'*Aowa.*' ('No.')

This was the song my granny and I sang all the way between our house and hers. I was not supposed to be exposed to the cold. Koko would put me on her back and cover me completely but this meant I could not see what was happening or how far we were, and so we sang the song. Though I was feeling sick, I enjoyed the trips on Koko's back. Although the name was not used, I also have another name that belongs to my granny. So Koko enjoyed looking after her namesake, and the two of us shared a special bond at the time.

My sicknesses were well known in the rural areas as diseases of the poor. Everyone believed these sicknesses were caused either by malnutrition or witchcraft. These explanations did not apply in my case – my family was well fed and we were also part of *batho ba ka setaseng* (the believers – those who went to church); we could not suffer sicknesses of the heathens. But I was no longer a bubbly little girl; I spent most of my time being treated for my illnesses. Daddy was coming home less frequently. My world was shattered.

Koko and Aunty Hunadi usually took it in turns to look after me and make sure I got to the clinic. On other days, my mother would send some of the older girls and boys from our school to take me to the clinic. I was puzzled by my weakness and only wanted to be normal and do what others did. I quietly observed all the things that were happening around me. One day Aunty Hunadi was getting herself ready to take me to the clinic. She thought I was sleeping and started washing herself in front of me. I was interested to see how she washed her private parts. I did not understand why Aunty Hunadi washed that way but I started imitating her when washing. That helped me a bit with the smell I now lived with most of the time – the smell I kept to myself and, like my other secret, never shared with anyone.

Throughout all of this, I continued to go to school when I felt strong and well and my schoolwork was very good. I enjoyed the privilege of having a mother as a teacher because she taught me things at home.

When I was in Standard One, I transferred to the same farm school that Matome and Angela had attended. Sipho had started there a year earlier. My health was better now and I started playing again, although I still bullied the other children.

School was about ten kilometres from home and we had to walk because there were no cars going in that direction. There was only one main road far from the village, so we walked on the narrow pedestrian path that was used to go to the fields. The path passed through the fields and during harvest time it was safe because there were many people working there.

We all enjoyed the walk. We would play along the way, the boys frequently teasing the girls. One of the games the boys played with the girls occurred mostly during hide-and-seek. It was one of the things the boys did to prove they were men. Although there was never penetration, the boys wanted to put their penises on the girls' genitals. It was called go robalana (having sex, to those who understood it).

Each day on the way home from school, one boy called Masilu would try to prove his manhood by propositioning me. When I refused repeatedly, he decided to show me what he was made of. On this particular day, Masilu chased me into the field behind the bushes and forced himself onto me. Masilu had 'sex' with me, although there was no penetration. The other boys in the group were cheering Masilu while I was fighting to get out from underneath him.

Eventually I managed to escape and ran back to the group feeling completely embarrassed. The others, who included my brother Sipho, laughed at me. Sipho did not defend me at all. Perhaps it was because he was a boy and he knew what boys did to girls in their quest to experiment with their manhood. Games like this happened often and the girls always ended up feeling embarrassed. It did not mean anything to the boys; it was their way of showing the girls they were men. To the girls, however, it was very embarrassing to undergo such humiliation while others cheered. But we knew it was an issue never to be discussed at home or in front of our elders.

As part of the recreational activities at school, young girls were chosen to be in the 'Wayfarers' group. They sang songs such as: '*Rena re thabile, rena re thabile, rena, re thabile ruri a rena le kgwara. Bangwe ke meleko, ba kwata ka pela, gab a tsebe melao ya mahlasetsana.*' ('We are happy, we are happy, we are happy, indeed we do not have any troubles. Others are troublemakers; they are short-tempered because they do not understand the rules and the ways of us little stars'.)

I wanted to forget the things that had happened to me and be like other girls and so I was happy to be chosen for the 'Wayfarers'. I sang the songs as loudly as my friends and I was proud of my uniform, a blue dress with a beret. We enjoyed the competitions that were held as we met girls from other schools.

The farm school did not have higher primary classes and after I had been there for a year, Sipho, our cousin Moyahabo and I moved back to the schools in the village. My sister Angela went to stay with our aunt in another village so that she could be closer to a good high school. At this point mother was managing on her own because one day my father went off to Johannesburg as normal, and never came back.

The family struggled to cope. We depended on our mother who was studying via distance learning to obtain a university degree to better her qualifications as a teacher. She travelled a good deal in the course of her studies – to Pretoria and other places, even overseas to Israel for Religious studies – often leaving us alone. She grew her own vegetables and because she was very busy, she hired a gardener named Bra Joe. Bra Joe was in his thirties, a nephew of one of the ladies my mother knew. He came to live with our family. His room was in the garage at the back but it had another door that gave him access to the house through the passage on the side of the bedrooms. He enjoyed staying with the family.

Apart from the family dog, Bra Joe was the only other creature I would find at home when I got back from school. I was ten years old, in Standard Three, and now that Angela was gone I always came home early so that I could cook. Bra Joe liked playing with me and calling me pet names. I did not like the games. Bra Joe would ask me to show him my underwear. I protested and refused but I never told my mother about our exchanges.

One night someone came into the bedroom which I shared with Sipho. My brother slept on the bed far from the door while I slept on the floor next to the door. The sound of heavy breathing woke me. Because I wet myself at night I was not allowed to sleep in a nightdress. I only wore my underwear.

'Hu, hu, hu', was a whispering sound made along with heavy breathing. There was a forceful push of something between my thighs into my vagina from the back, and I felt some cold fluid that accompanied another heavy 'Hu, hu, hu'.

The sweaty odour of a heavy, labouring person and the thick thing in between my thighs making its way into my vagina from behind made me scream.

'*Ijo, mmawee!*' ('Mommy, please help!')

When I felt the coldness of the fluids I screamed even louder and the man quickly left the room. When my mother arrived to see why I was screaming, he was already gone, and she told me it must have been a bad dream. In the house, our bedroom door was never closed or locked. The night light coming through the passage window made the room lighter and it had been easy for me to recognise Bra Joe as he rushed out of the room. He was not wearing anything.

More than anything, it was the fluids I recognised and the penis pushing itself into my vagina. The heavy breathing and the wetness were frighteningly familiar. I knew I was never going to be safe anywhere again – not in my home, not while walking back from school, not in my own village or community. The incident was never discussed or mentioned again and the confusion in my mind expanded.

But I had to play *kgati* with my friends like I had managed to do before. I had to pass my maths tests; I had to do recitations in my mother tongue; and I had to play the *mmasekitlana* (a storytelling game where beautiful stones are used in a dialogue situation). *Mmasekitlana* was only played by girls and we would demonstrate our understanding of life and the happenings around us. Often girls would have a family illustrated by the use of two medium-sized stones (to represent the parents) and a number of small ones (the children). Each girl had a story to tell, but one storyline that was common was the one where the father and mother had to sleep on top of each other, with the father always on top. Our storylines indicated that we were aware of sex but we did not understand what it meant and the details around it. The small stones would be sleeping in the same house with the parents and

14

watching while they had sex. My *mmasekitlana* stories also often featured fathers who worked in Johannesburg and never came home. I was trying to express and understand the things that had happened in my life, was trying to see if what I had experienced was 'normal' to other people too.

I was still 'mommy's little angel in the blue train', but at age ten I had to watch the way I sat. I made sure I imitated Aunty Hunadi even more when I bathed my private parts. The stains on my underwear did not disappear. I was no longer a free little girl; just like all girls, I had to start learning how to live in my environment by observation. I kept my silence and watched my mother deal with the tragedy of my sister's accident.

One day, on her way to school, Angela was hit by a car while crossing in front of the school bus from which she had just alighted. Her body was thrown over the top of the bus to the other side of the road and she had to be hospitalised for a long time. I was sad about my sister. Although we were not close, Angela used to bake cookies for us. She was the quiet one in the family and spent most of her time with our aunts. When she eventually came home, she used crutches to walk. Angela's situation seemed more pressing than my fluids.

I let my mother look after Angela and excelled in my school-work in order to receive attention and mask the sadness I was feeling inside. I wrote other children's homework for them and knew every recitation and poem we did at school. I was loved by all my teachers and many children wanted to be around me so that I could help them with their homework. In my mother's eyes, I was her bright little girl. In my siblings' and cousins' eyes, I was a spoilt brat. It was the beginning of my descent into the darkness of secrecy.

While Angela was still recovering from her accident, my mother had to leave home again. She was deployed to a district far away from our village to a school that was short of teachers.

My older brother Matome was now at a teacher's training college, also far away from home, so I had to adjust to living at home with a woman named MmaLethabo whom mother had hired as a nanny for Sipho and I. Sipho was entering his teens and he was not a good boy. Like the rest of the boys in the village, he was busy experimenting with sex and cigarettes; he would come home very late and his schoolwork was deteriorating.

Angela was finally walking but her foot appeared to be permanently damaged and she had a slight limp. Life was tough for her – she was in Matric and under pressure to pass, and she could not look after Sipho and me.

Matome had proved he was a responsible young man. He had passed his Matric and was now in his last year of teacher training. The profession of teaching was highly regarded in the community, along with nursing and the police service. I, in particular, loved the situation because it strengthened the respect other children had for our family – we had a mother who was a teacher and who had been overseas as part of her studies, and now a brother who was about to qualify as a teacher.

To celebrate Matome's graduation, my mother decided to give a large party. My cousins and I were very excited as she sent us around to distribute invitation cards to the rest of the village. It was the first time in my life my family had given a party. The men put up a marquee and later in the week a special cow would be slaughtered. All the women of the village came to help with the baking and the preparations. Everyone at school knew there would be eating at my home so I was the centre of attention. At the end of the week, there were lots of cookies, home-made beer and other liquor in our garage for the celebration.

Relatives from far away started arriving on Friday for the events. Early on Saturday morning all the family members left in a hired minibus to go to Matome's college to attend the graduation ceremony. The proceedings in the hall were exciting for my cousins and I. We were also intrigued by the many graduates wearing their ceremonial dress – 'academic regalia' was a new phrase that I learned. After the ceremony, we gathered in the garden of the college campus to take pictures with my brother who made us so proud.

Back at home, the ladies were dressed in identical aprons and dresses, which were specially made for them as part of the celebration. It was a custom in the community for the ladies who were involved in the cooking and preparation for celebrations, weddings, unveilings of tombstones, and so on, to have a uniform. They prepared a feast of food. When we arrived home in the minibus, it had to stop on the streets so that the crowds could sing and ululate for the graduate.

Koko praised her first grandson who was now also the first graduate in the family. The family name and the entire clan were praised for having raised a responsible young man who had made them proud. Then the entourage moved into the marquee, which was beautifully decorated with flowers and tablecloths. Delicious food and drinks were put on the tables for the graduate, his friends and the many distinguished guests. Matome's former high school principal was the guest-speaker. He spoke very highly of Matome and expressed his pride in him and his achievements. Everyone enjoyed the occasion. The entire village and people from the neighbouring villages came to celebrate with the family, although it seemed to me that they came mainly to eat and get drunk.

3

It was the beginning of a new school term. My friends and I had made it through Standard Five and we were going into high school. Since there was only one secondary school close by, we knew we would all still be together. It was situated between two villages, so we would also have children from the other village joining us.

My mother's cousin, Lesiba, came to live with us and the house was now full with the nanny, Sipho, Matome (who had returned home), Lesiba and another boy from distant relations. I was the only girl in the house. Our lives ranged from playing separate games to fighting furiously. Sipho still did not approve of his baby sister, mainly because at school I was always one of the top students, and since he had managed to fail two years, we were now in Standard Six together. The teachers always told him about my performance and how disappointed they were in him by comparison. Our mother was also not happy with the situation since she knew that Sipho had the potential to be a bright pupil. She had no idea that my brilliant performance was due to my undying desire for attention, or that Sipho's poor marks were one of the after-effects of the games he and the boys played as part of their experimenting escapades. Now he had more male company so the games became their way of excluding me from the 'men's world' as he liked to tell me.

I took pride in knowing I was regarded as a bright student. If I was lucky, I might do Accountancy, which I had heard was a very interesting subject. I would also be in the drum majorettes because I would be favoured. After all, I was the daughter of one of the village's teachers. In high school we were to be introduced to subjects such as Accountancy, Business Economics, General Science, Physical Science, Agriculture, Needlework and Housecraft, Mathematics and Typing. The Standard Six pupils were divided into two groups since the school was just two years old and there were not many teachers and classrooms. It only had seven classrooms, one staff room and the principal's office.

'Line up girls and boys, and put out your hands so I can see your fingers.' That was Mistress Maupi, the Accountancy and Typing teacher.

'She is not a very nice person,' whispered one of the girls. 'She speaks very funny.'

My friends, Dalia, Mmabatho and Dikeledi, and I were too excited on our first day in high school to respond to her. We did not have time to listen to people who had failed classes. The four of us were chosen for the Commerce class because we all had long fingers and that meant we could type, which was how students were allocated into different classes and subject groupings. If you were not chosen for the Commerce class, it meant you were going to do Agriculture or Needlework. None of us wanted to do either of those subjects. Agriculture was for boys and Needlework was considered to be a subject for those who were less intelligent.

The activities at high school were exciting. My friends and I had become very close over the years. We shared food and played together, although I was excluded from playing netball because I was not a sporty person. Fortunately, my teachers liked me and I was introduced into the debating world, which I loved because it allowed me to be the centre of attention. Our weekly debate topics ranged from: 'Corporal punishment at school must be abolished' to

'Euthanasia must be abolished'. We relied on our older siblings to help us formulate arguments around the topics. It was easy for me. Now that he was a qualified teacher, Matome was there for me, and sometimes my mother would help. I regarded my debating as a high-calibre pastime, only for the bright and clever students.

Apart from being in the debating team, I had played the king's daughter-in-law in a drama in primary school. I loved acting and was proud that I could remember my part as well as all the other actors' words. I couldn't wait to perform for my mother when she came home on weekends to check on us. I made my mother proud, and that made my relationship with Sipho even more sour.

There were other activities and school trips in which I took part, including sporting trips. Everyone went to cheer the school's soccer and netball teams. I was convinced that, unlike the drama and debating competition trips, the sports trips were not for the bright and intelligent. There is one soccer and netball trip that I will never forget because it reinforced my opinion that participation in the debate and drama team was only for the bright and intelligent, like me.

The school went to Mussina for the games. On our way back, the bus stopped so that we could get something to drink and eat. The place in which we stopped was an Afrikaans area in which we had to speak either Afrikaans or English. This was difficult because prior to high school most of our subjects were taught in our mother tongue and there were few opportunities for us to learn other languages, Afrikaans and English in particular. Only a few pupils, especially those who were in the debating team, had had the chance to practise their English. The only exposure to English that all students had was in short stories and poetry. In Afrikaans, we were taught recitations, *opstel* (composition) and *briewe* (letters).

On this particular day, when the bus stopped to allow us to buy food and drink, the store owner told the teachers that he would appreciate it if we (the children) would go into the store in groups of five. Then he could monitor us and ensure we were not stealing anything from the shop. The first group that went in was ours and it contained one of the girls from the Needlework class. On her way out, the girl, Mokgadi, was stopped by the shop owner who spoke to her in Afrikaans, claiming that she had not paid for the things she was carrying.

'*Hoekom het jy nie vir die dinge betaal nie?*' ('Why didn't you pay for the things you've got?') The big, angry Afrikaner store owner shook the girl as he waited for an answer.

He had been standing at the shop entrance while his partner stood by the cash registers. The store owner probably did not see Mokgadi pay for the can of cooldrink and packet of chips she held in her hands. Although she had the change to prove she had paid, she was now forced to explain the situation to the store owner in either English or Afrikaans.

'*Ke mpayile hle sir, change se,*' she answered in a mixture of English and her home language, meaning, 'I did buy sir, and here is the change to prove that I did pay for the things.'

The man could not understand her so he kept shaking her and pushing her out of the shop. The teachers saw what was happening and came hurrying off the bus to rescue her. She was in tears, unable to explain herself in either English or Afrikaans. The teachers apologised to the angry shop owner and we were all told to leave the shop and get onto the bus.

On Monday, the incident was reported to the school principal. He made poor Mokgadi stand in front of the whole school during the morning assembly and the entire school was forced to speak English for the day so that we could learn.

Incidents such as this did not stop the school from sending us on trips – we went to Durban, Venda, Mussina and into our town of Pietersburg. There were also trips that we could undertake individually or in a group, depending on the distance, to those places that used to hold trade exhibition shows and entertainment activities in the District. The annual Easter Shows were held at the Lebowakgomo Showground and the Mokomene Showground. Children went there to play, view the exhibition stalls and enjoy many other things. The shows would run for a week and on those days school finished early so that children could attend the shows.

'Naomi and Mosibudi, please can you come with me to my mother's friend's house? I believe it is not far, just on the other side of the Showground. We can walk and if it is late they can take us home because they have a car.'

That was me asking the two girls with whom I had come to the Showground to accompany me on a family visit. My mother had made many friends in all sorts of places during the course of her work and studies. The girls agreed to go with me and I promised them we would be given food since we were all hungry. This particular Showground was about twenty-five kilometres away from our village, and the three of us had travelled by bus to get there.

We started to walk to the Mpshanas' house but after a while we realised we were lost. We saw three older women walking on the other side of the road.

'Realotsha bomma, re be re kgopela go botsisa gore ge re eya ka ga Mpshana re sepela bjane. Re lahlegile ka gore ga re dule mo. Re tlile ka Showground bjale re tswerwe ke tlala.' ('Greetings our elders, we wanted to know if you could help us by showing us the way to the Mpshanas' home. We think we are lost since we are not familiar with this village. We came to the Showground and now we want to get to the Mpshanas' to get food.')

I spoke to the ladies since I was the one who knew the family we were going to visit.

'Aowa, bana baka, ga le ya lahlega kudu,' replied one of the ladies. ('No, my children, you are not entirely lost.')

'Hey, Ephraim, please come here. These three children here are on their way to the Mpshanas' and since you work there, can you please take them there? We could help them but since we are on our way to the other side of the village, you will be able to help them.'

She was talking to a young man in his late twenties who was walking past carrying a crate of beers on his head. He had a beard, looked half-drunk and was very dirty. He happily offered to show us the way.

'Go lokile bana baka le tla tloga le bo malome a lena se bauwe. Baya go tseba ebile ba bereka go hlatswa dikoloi tsa ka gona,' the ladies said, taking another direction. ('It's okay my children, you will be accompanied by your uncle here. He knows exactly where you are going since he works there washing the family cars.')

We gratefully thanked the three ladies and joined the young man. We heard that his name was Ephraim and he told us not to be scared of him at all; we would get to our destination, 'just like those old ladies said'.

After about ten minutes, he asked us to carry the crate for him as a favour in return for him taking us to the Mpshanas' house. Naomi and I carried the crate between us.

Then he added, 'As a matter of fact, I need you girls to walk in front of me. I must be able to check you out and see who amongst you is fit and has a big behind.'

Ephraim instructed us, 'Don't be terrified, wa marago a magolo ke yena e tlilego go ba mosadi wa ka naase wo' ('the one with a big behind will be my woman today').

Frightened, we did as we were told.

Whistling admiringly, he said, 'Si, si, si, ijoo, ngwana a tla a paka.' ('This child is so fit.') 'You, walk on the other side of your friends. In fact, why don't you carry the beer crate on your head just like women do? I need to have a good view of your behind. It is normally so beautiful when a woman is carrying something on her head.'

24

He said this as he pointed to Mosibudi who, although like us was twelve, was a little fitter and better endowed than Naomi and I. Mosibudi's eyes started getting wet with tears, but she had no choice other than to obey. As for the crate, we were all used to carrying buckets of water and wood on our heads, so it was no problem at all. Mosibudi's tears were tears of fear at the thought of what she was going to have to go through as the man's 'woman' for the day.

'Let's run away. I'm scared,' Naomi whispered to me as we were helping Mosibudi put the crate on her head.

'No, I don't think that's a good idea. We have to stick together and wait until Mosibudi is released. I can't run and leave her behind alone; I was the one who asked the two of you to come with me. I will walk with her until we are released. You can run if you want to,' I answered, feeling responsible for our trip.

While we helped Mosibudi with the crate, Naomi made a run for it and managed to get away. Ephraim shouted after her, 'You can go since you are not as fit as she is!'

Now the trip was tense for Mosibudi and I as we felt helpless and terrified. At least, we thought, we would still make it to the Mpshanas' house. When we met other people on the road, Ephraim told them that he was in the company of two beautiful girls. None of the passers-by noticed or reacted to the terror on our faces. They simply walked past.

'Now girls, the Mpshanas' home is that one over there. You see those two big white houses and a thatched rondavel? It is there you are supposed to be going. It even looks like they are home because the car is there in the yard. However, it is unfortunate that you will not be going there right now. We must first go to my house so that I and my woman can finish our thing. As for you, I will have to find my friend so that you can be a pair,' Ephraim said to me.

We did not respond to his conversation, but we walked along obediently as we did not know where we were being taken and what was going to happen to us. It was getting late and we realised we could no longer go back to the Showground.

Eventually we got to a house. Most of the yards in the villages were not fenced; this house had two thatched rondavels facing each other and one four-cornered house in the middle. All the houses were built with soil. Since we were in front of Ephraim, he told us to walk into the *mosha* (an African veranda built with soil and stones which is the front area that connects all the houses in the yard). This is a wall that has two entrances, one at the back and one in the front of the yard. All the houses in the villages had the same thing, mainly to prevent dust from getting into the house and to ensure there was a reception area for visitors before they went into the house.

He instructed Mosibudi to put the crate down on the veranda and told her to open the door of the rondavel on the left. He seemed to have forgotten about finding his friend for me, but told me to sit and wait at the small sitting place that was built alongside the walling *bolele* (a short wall around the long one that is used as the veranda, designed so that people can sit on it instead of using chairs while waiting or resting on the veranda). I sat down alongside the wall and watched as Mosibudi, without protesting but with tears in her eyes, did as she was told. Then Ephraim followed her inside the rondavel and locked the door behind him.

'*Mmawee, le ya mpolaya, ke nyaka go ya gae!*' ('You are hurting me, I want to go home!') Mosibudi was screaming and I could hear she was struggling.

'Hey, sit still and keep quiet before I cut your throat with this knife,' Ephraim said in a loud, irritated voice.

'*Mmawee!*' (Mommy!')

Now Mosibudi's cry was becoming painful for me to listen to. I stood up to see if I could see anything. It was not a very good door so I managed to see what was going on through the cracks.

It all looked so familiar – I recognised what was being done to my friend. I saw Ephraim's half-naked body on top of Mosibudi and the scene made me run. I ran out of the yard and into the street to look for help. There was a woman coming towards me.

'Mma (Auntie), there is a man in that house who has my friend inside and he is busy!' I started crying and could not finish or bring myself to say what I was supposed to tell the woman. Finally I managed to explain to her how we had walked there and begged her to come with me so that we could help Mosibudi.

As it happened, the woman knew the house very well for she was Ephraim's eldest sister. She told me she would come with me but cautioned, 'I am afraid I cannot help you, little girl. The man you are talking about is my brother and he is a very dangerous person. Is he drunk?' asked the woman.

'I think so; he was carrying a crate of beers which are there next to the house,' I told her.

I strongly believed that the woman knew what her younger brother was up to. She was old enough to understand what he could be doing with a young girl in the house. We walked into the yard again and as we approached the rondavel, she called out to her brother: 'Ephraim, o dira eng ngwana wa batho, mo bulele ba tloge.' ('Ephraim, what are you doing to the poor child? Please open the door so the girls can leave.')

There was no answer. After about five long minutes, the door finally opened. Ephraim was wearing only his pants and his belt was not fastened. Then Mosibudi came out of the rondavel. Her eyes and face were swollen; she had been crying for a long time, and her school uniform was wrinkled. She must have been struggling but she was silent. She was also not walking properly and was clearly in pain. The woman looked at her and shook her head. Ephraim was now looking embarrassed and sober but he did not show any remorse. He was not happy with his sister's presence either. He walked past me and his sister with an angry face and went outside the veranda to the back of the yard.

27

The woman told us to go home. She said there was nothing she could do to help us. I took Mosibudi's hand and we walked out of the wall back to the road. We did not talk for a while.

'*O go dirile eng?*' I asked Mosibudi at last. ('What did he do to you?') Although I had heard Mosibudi's screams and knew exactly what had happened, I thought asking her would break the ice.

'Nothing,' answered Mosibudi. Her eyes were still red and swollen. I kept quiet; I knew what had happened. Not only did her eyes and face speak volumes, her slight struggle to walk properly confirmed it all. We walked in silence for a long time until we could get to the main road where we were supposed to catch a bus back to our village. As there was no bus in sight we decided to hitch-hike to the taxi rank.

A car stopped because someone in it recognised me. 'Hey there, Sipho's younger sister, come let's give you a ride home. Where have you girls been? The activities at the show ended a long time ago. Come, jump in, we will drop you off at the bus station so that you can catch the bus to your village.'

I recognised Segopotso, my brother Sipho's friend from another village.

Relieved, we got into the car that had three occupants in it – Segopotso, who was about five years older than me, and two men who looked a bit older than him.

He asked us why we were heading home so late because the other children who had been to the show had gone home some time ago. Mosibudi was lost in her own world and could not speak. I told Segopotso we had had to go somewhere first. I could not tell him the truth.

One of the older men in the car said, '*Re tshwanetse go ba re le lucky, Modimo ga a fe ka letsogo, basadi ba babotse so?*' ('We must be the lucky ones today. Such pretty women. Indeed God does not always give you things directly. He sometimes kicks it to you.')

28

I knew what it meant when a man or a boy called you *mosadi o mo botse* (a pretty woman): you were his object of desire.

'But you, Segopotso, you are my brother's friend. I am sure he is not going to appreciate the fact that you sold his sister to your uncles,' I appealed to Segopotso, who was looking excited by his companion's statement.

'*Ah, mara bo uncle ba ka ge ba nyaka basadi nna ke reng. Gona bjale re le file lift, selo se le ka se dirang gore leboga ke gore le ngwatise bo uncle. Or, bjang bo nono's?*' answered Segopotso, while brushing Mosibudi's face. ('Oh, what do you think I should do if my uncles want to have pretty women? Right now we have given you a lift in our car. The least you can do to show your gratitude will be to give yourselves to my uncles.')

Irritated I responded, 'If that's the case, then you can stop the car and let us get off right here. We did not know that you gave us a lift so that we could repay you in that manner. We will use the money I have from sweets I sold for my mother at school this morning. We will catch the bus home.'

Angrily the driver pulled off the road and he shouted: '*Fotsek, tsamayang dikobo ke lena!*' ('*Voetsak* [Get lost], you can go, you ugly things!')

Luckily, as we got out of the car a bus came along. We got on it and eventually arrived home after seven. Mosibudi and I parted company at the bus stop. As soon as I arrived home I told my mother what had happened. I needed to give her an explanation for my late homecoming and I wanted to share Mosibudi's ordeal.

'Ma, while at the Showground today, Mosibudi and I along with this other girl felt very hungry and I thought we should go to the Mpshanas' to get something to eat. Unfortunately we never got there.'

'What happened? Why didn't you get there?' asked my mother, a woman with a very strict approach to bringing up her children. She never wanted us to get away with anything, tried to make sure we did not behave badly, and always punished us for naughty behaviour. She was a very authoritarian woman and embraced her cultural values of not being too friendly with her children for fear that we would not know who the parent was. I was scared of her. Even my mother's seven siblings, of whom she was the eldest, were terrified of her authority. She commanded respect.

I told the whole story and my mother was very angry. Not only did she know Mosibudi's parents, she was distantly related to Mosibudi's mother. She immediately phoned her friend Mma-Mpshana and related the story.

Mother explained the whole incident as I had told it to her and informed MmaMpshana that since she knew Mosibudi's parents and they were her relatives, she would have to go their house to find out how they were handling the matter.

She went to Mosibudi's home. When she came back, she told me that Mosibudi's parents didn't know what to do since she refused to talk to them; she simply cried. They could not take the matter anywhere. It was to remain a family secret.

MmaMpshana said the only thing she could do was to fire Ephraim.

That did not help Mosibudi's pain. On Monday at school she avoided me at all costs. I knew I had to keep the secret to protect her although I took comfort from the fact that at least her parents knew what had happened. But inside I felt even more confused as I now wondered if this was how relations were supposed to be between men and women, boys and girls. I had experienced and seen enough to suggest that forced encounters were the norm. Although Mosibudi had struggled slightly to walk properly, by the time we had reached home she had improved, and I sensed that it had not been her first time. I was also convinced there had been no bleeding at all.

I was even more confused and puzzled when one day my cousin Winnifred told me about a conversation she had overheard between her younger sister Khomotso and a friend.

Khomotso was apparently relating an incident that had happened to her without noticing that Winnifred was listening nearby.

'You know, this guy Shadrack thinks he is clever. Two days ago on the night before Rangata's funeral, after our choir had sung at the night vigil, I was walking back home alone after I parted ways with Lebo at the corner when he approached me. He started telling me how much he had always wanted me, and then he reached to grab my arm and started twisting it around. When I told him to leave me alone, he told me how he was going to show me that I would never run away from him. He was going to "have" me that night. He had always wanted me so badly. He forced me to sleep with him.'

Winnie walked into the room to confront her sister about the incident before she heard the rest of the story. She threatened to tell their mother if Khomotso did not tell her the entire incident from start to end. Knowing that her mother disapproved of her singing in the choir and would punish her, Khomotso had to tell Winnie the truth, though she begged her not to tell their mother who was working in Johannesburg and not living with them. In those days girls participated in choirs that were hired to sing at funerals and weddings. Khomotso was a member of the choir against her mother's wishes. On the day that Shadrack had forced himself on her, she was with the choir at a night vigil, which was always held on a Friday night before a funeral.

Khomotso admitted that Shadrack had slept with her at the corner on the ground that night, 'not raped, but he slept with me'. Like all the other girls, she did not know that it was called 'rape' if she did not consent to it. She also was too young to have 'sex'. Winnie and I recalled that on that evening, Khomotso had come home with sand and dry grass in the hair at the back of her head. I had actually asked her why she was in such a mess and she arrogantly told me, 'Mind your business. You do not have a child my age.'

Winnie went to phone their mother who came back the following weekend to punish Khomotso. She was beaten badly and had to promise she would never go back to the choir. As for Shadrack, Khomotso's mother went to his home and hit him in front of his parents. She was so angry that she did not even tell his parents why she was there. The minute she saw him, she jumped at him like an angry bull and hit him with the *sjambok* (whip) she had taken with her. It was the end of Khomotso's singing but she had to move on with her life just like the rest of us.

The incident was never mentioned by anyone again. It was a *khupamarama* – which comes from the Sepedi proverb *koma re bolla kgororwane, khupamarama re hwa nayo* (we only talk about the initiation but we take the secret of what happens there with us to the grave) – like everybody else's. The boys continued to experiment. The girls were becoming young women. The villagers continued to drink home-made beer, marula beer and Black Label. Everyone carried on with their lives.

Back at school, Lethabo, one of the girls in my class, started rushing out in the middle of lessons to throw up. She was making a habit of it. She had also stopped playing netball for which she had been the team's coach. In the village, she would hide when the others were playing drum majorettes and other games.

One day our Accountancy teacher, Mistress Maupi, commented sarcastically while Lethabo was out vomiting: 'Girls, you see what happens when instead of studying at night you play around with boys? These are the consequences of your behaviour.' Obviously, Mistress Maupi knew exactly what was happening with Lethabo.

Some months later, the class found out why she had thrown up so much; she was going to be a fifteen-year-old mother.

4

Sipho and I moved to a better high school about fifteen kilometres away from our village to do Standard Eight. Angela had gone to college to follow in our big brother's footsteps and qualify as a teacher. I enjoyed my new school; my cousin Moyahabo was in my class and I made some new friends – Tshidi, Mahlodi, Sophia and Kgaugelo – because Dalia, Mmabatho and Dikeledi had stayed on at my old school. I continued with my Commerce subjects and Sipho was in the General class. He seemed to like Agriculture particularly. Our brother, Matome, was a qualified Agriculture teacher who happened to teach at the school, and we both attained some status because of our brother's presence.

Eight other children from my village also went to the school. Sipho and I now had company on the walk back home. In the morning we caught a bus but it did not run after school. I was a big girl now. Though we still had a nanny, who had changed a number of times, I had learnt to clean the house, cook and iron my brother's white shirts. I enjoyed being the little mommy while my sister was at college. I was doing well at school; I would because my mother did not expect me to disappoint her now that she had accepted Sipho's average schoolwork.

He was becoming a young man, learning *tsotsi-taal* (a mixture of different languages deemed to be a disrespectful way of talking) and continuing with the games he and the boys in the community played to experiment with life. He began to protest at having to share a room with our nanny and I. Khomotso was the only relative staying with us now because she had to help with the household chores and her mother thought she should have her schoolwork supervised by her aunt. Our other relatives had gone back to their homes since it was becoming difficult for the family to accommodate everyone, particularly with Angela's newborn baby now in the house. Angela had come back from her first year at college very pregnant and a baby girl was born soon afterwards.

Everyone was happy there was a new life because in our community the child of an unwed mother belongs to her family. All of the girls in our house had to help since Angela had to go back to college to finish her studies. The baby helped to ease the loss that same year of my mother's great-grandmother who had been such a pillar of strength.

New schools were being built in the villages and Matome moved to teach at another school. My mother also came back to teach nearby. She completed her degree and we held a big party – a duplicate of Matome's – to celebrate. I felt that life was beginning to shape up because everyone was back at home.

At the party, I overheard something I carried with me for a long time. My mother's two female cousins, Aunt Mmakgoro and Aunt Mosima were talking about their sister who was married and having marital problems. Apparently their sister's husband drank too much beer and he would beat her up.

'Who does she think she is? What was she thinking, getting married anyway? In this family, we do not get married. Marriage is not in our genes. We were cursed a long time ago by our ancestors. Can't she look around and see that all our cousins are not married? Those who tried, their husbands left them. She is really trying our ancestors' patience. Even our daughters will not get married,' remarked Aunt Mmakgoro.

'You are right but you know how stubborn our sister is. Her husband will continue to abuse and ill-treat her because she does not have the blessings from our ancestors since they did not give us a gift as far as marriage is concerned. She must be thinking we are fools because we are not getting married,' added Aunt Mosima.

Even at the young age of thirteen, I understood the conversation very well. I was familiar with the language and terms of references used by the elders. I looked around me. My two cousins were already single mothers. My sister Angela and all my aunts were single parents. Although I had felt unfortunate after my father had left – when my friends such as Dalai and Dikeledi still had their fathers – I knew that none of the children in my family called anyone father. My grandmother raised us in her home; we were one big family with too many grandchildren. The conversation I overheard appeared to confirm the truth about our family.

This life was all I knew – people moving around a lot, sex, drunk adults and stories of witchcraft. I was full of questions and there were no answers anywhere. In that same year I graduated into being a young woman when I started my periods.

I had not heard much about periods before. Then, one day at school, the female teachers wanted to check if all the girls were washing their underwear properly. This was part of the health education routine, and was not performed very thoroughly. All the girls were asked to line up and pull up our school dresses for the teachers to see if there was a map of urine on our panties. A lot of children wet themselves at night and a map would mean you were untidy and you would be told to wash yourself properly.

On this day I was standing behind a girl who was already sixteen. She had blood on her panties, not a map of urine. All I knew was that the girl was *o ya mensa*, meaning 'she is menstruating'. We gossiped about it but we never really knew what it meant.

Unfortunately, my periods were accompanied by terrible abdominal pains and I had to tell Angela and Moyahabo why I spent the whole day sleeping and crying. They had both started their periods already and told me to ask my mother for sanitary towels. I had been using toilet paper because I did not know what else to use.

'You must know that this means if you sleep with a boy, you will have a child.' This was all I got from my mother when I asked for sanitary towels.

The following day she told me that since I was suffering with abdominal pain, I should come with her to see the doctor. I waited outside while my mother spoke to the doctor in his consulting room. Then he called me in and told me he would give me tablets that I should take for three months and then I should return for more. He never even gave me a check-up. I thought it was because I was bleeding and he did not want to see the blood. I asked if the tablets would take away my pain and he assured me they would.

In the taxi on the way home, the terrible pain continued but my mother told me that all girls experience pain with their periods at first. She also told me not to forget that I must go back to the doctor for more tablets when this supply was finished. The next day at school, curious as to why I had not been in class on the previous day, Tshidi, who was older than all of us in the group, asked me where I had been. I told them about my periods and the pain I suffered. I also spoke about my visit to the doctor. Tshidi knew more about sex and contraceptives than the rest of us. She asked me to describe the tablets because she thought she knew them. She had been given them after her miscarriage so that she did not fall pregnant again.

'Ah, the doctor gave you contraceptive pills,' she commented. 'I know them because the nurses at the health centre gave them

36

to me. They told me they are for family planning. Your mother took you for family planning without telling you.'

This puzzled me because I knew I was not sleeping with anyone. The closest I had come so far to having a boyfriend was when George, who was very popular with girls in the class because he was the younger brother of one of the female teachers, had proposed to me. But I could not go out with him because he was already seeing Sophia, one of the girls in our group. There had been other encounters but they were just boys experimenting with me and I never thought it was a big deal since most girls went through the same thing.

I was very upset with my mother for tricking me but I didn't dare tell her how betrayed I felt. After one month of taking the pills every day in the hope that I would not have more abdominal pain with my periods, I decided to stop. Each day, instead of swallowing the pill, I would throw it away. My mother did not check on me because she thought that the lie the doctor had told me would stand for a long time.

I was even angrier when I realised my abdominal pains were getting worse. I was always absent from school for the three days of my period. One day my grandmother told me that the pain meant I was a woman and all I needed to do was stay strong. However, she promised she was going to mix a *muti* (a herbal mixture) for me to help minimise the pain.

I was busy at my new school and was exposed to many new experiences. '*Khutsi, khutsi, rena re yo ikhutsa, amen, halleluya, amen, halleluya, amen. Bootswa, rena re yo ikhutsa amen, halleluya, amen, halleluya, amen, halleluya.*' ('Rest, rest, we are going to find rest. Amen, Hallelujah, Amen. Hallelujah, Amen. Adultery and all the bad things will be taken away from us. Amen, Hallelujah, Amen.') This song was sung by a group of crusaders and their pastor who came to our school to preach the gospel and convert the sinners. They called themselves Born Again Christians and were sent by God to redeem the sinners and attract young children to Jesus Christ. Their singing was accompanied by guitars, drums and pianos. All the children from the village would pack into the school halls and dance to the music. There was also a big marquee in the fields where evening worship services were held.

'*Morena Jesu o rile, etlang bohle ba le lapisitswqeng. Bale imelwang ke melato le dibe tsa lena, e tlang gonna. Ke tla le hlatswa le sheufale bjale ka leswena.*' ('If you are frightened and feeling sinful and dirty, God wants you. He wants to make you completely new and reformed. All you need to do is to accept that Jesus Christ is your Lord and Saviour. He died on the cross for you so that you can be saved. He will redeem you and make you a completely new creature.')

This was part of the pastor's sermon on the day my friend Tebogo and I attended the service. The choir sang in the middle of the sermon and then the pastor continued, '*Bao le lapisitsweng ke dibe le bootswa. Le se sa itseba, Morena Jesu o bitsa lena. Etlang go yena le nnweng sedibeng sa bophelo. Madi a gagwe a tshologile sefapanong gore le tle le be le bophelo bjo bo botse. Re tlile go rapela, gee le gore o ikwa o tshilafetse mme o lahlegile, etla ka pele o amogele Morena Jesu. Re tliel go rapela le wena gomme bophelo bja gago go tloga lehono bo tliele go fetoga.*' ('Those of you who are tired of your sins of promiscuity and adultery. Those of you who are lost and hurt. Those who are broke and poor. The Lord Jesus Christ is calling you. Come to Him those who are weary. Come and drink from the rivers of living waters. His blood was shed on the cross of Calvary for you so that you can have a better life and see the light. As we get to the end of our sermon for this afternoon, I am going to call on those of you who heard this message of life. Come to the front so that I can pray with you. Come and accept Jesus Christ as your Lord and Saviour. In order to have this new life with Jesus Christ, you must be Born Again. You will be new creatures from today. Come sister, come brother. The Lord is calling upon you.')

Now the pastor was calling on people to come to the front so that he could close the sermon by praying for them.

'Let's go, my friend,' I whispered to Tebogo. We both went; people were weeping and crying with their hands raised to the sky and the choir was singing.

'*Se mphete wena ya rategang, moloki wa ka, ga o ntse o thusa ba bangwe Morena, se mphete le nna. Jesu, Jesu, Jesu, Morena Jesu, Jesu wa ka keya go rapela, keya go rapela, ga o ntse o thusa ba bangwe, Morena, se mphete le nna.*' ('Please Lord Jesus, the beloved one. Do not pass me by when you save and help others. I pray Lord Jesus, please do not pass me by when you save and help others.')

The words were comforting to me. I felt as though I had found refuge and comfort in the Saviour. Many other girls were coming to the front as well, all crying with their hands lifted up.

The pastor and his support team prayed for us and we said a conversion prayer that welcomed Jesus Christ into our lives. We were told that we did not have to do anything – just by praying, our past sins were forgiven; we were new creatures and the children of God. We could now walk around proud to be Born Again. The other brothers and sisters who were already Born Again would help us through the journey. The ministry consisted of a group of young women, called ushers and counsellors, who were already Born Again so they knew what the 'new converts' would go through.

After the prayer, they came to hug and welcome the new converts into the ministry as God's children. My other friends, Tshidi, Sophia, Mahlodi and Kgaugelo had already been Born Again because the crusaders had been to their village first. This type of religion was new to me as I had always been to the Lutheran Church with my family. At night we were taught to study the Bible and say a prayer before going to bed. I knew a lot about God and Jesus Christ. We learnt about them at Sunday school classes and at school we held morning prayers before going to classes. I had also learnt about faith in Religious Education at both lower and higher primary school. I had acted in a religious drama at school, recited Psalms, and I knew many different scriptures.

This time around, though, I felt I needed this Saviour to come and save me. My world was lonely and scary and the Saviour seemed like the only person able to help me. I had been offered a chance to become new, so I started attending Sunday services at the tent and stopped going to my family's church. My mother was very upset because she did not believe that there was anything wrong with the way we prayed and worshipped. She had been to Israel; she knew a lot about Jesus Christ and his teachings, but she did not believe in the Born Again sect. She told me to stop going to the services but the pastors at the ministry had told us we would experience prejudice from our families and those who did not know about Jesus Christ. So what I was experiencing at home was not in isolation. The pastors comforted me and told me to pray for my mother so that she would see the light. In the evenings we held prayer services and Bible study lessons. We were taught to eat, sleep and preach the gospel of Jesus Christ. We were told we would be better people and we would one day go to paradise and dance with Jesus Christ for there was manna and khwiris waiting for the saved ones in heaven. The devil would never touch us again.

The following year I had to repeat my Matric (Standard Ten) because I hadn't got a university exemption. My mother told me it was because of all the time I spent at church and evening services. I needed an exemption because I did not want to go to teacher training college like my brother and sister. I wanted to be a 'Chartered Accountant' – the only respectful and good career I knew of since I was in the Commerce class. I also told my mother I wanted to go to a university far away from home – maybe to Johannesburg, Durban or Cape Town. There was no doubt I would make it; I was a good student and mother found me a private tutor who helped me with my Mathematics on Saturdays. Sipho was also repeating his matric as he had failed completely.

Things in my life shifted from too much worry to too much seeking refuge in the church. My mother had given up trying to stop me from going to the Born Again church and she was beginning to accommodate the crusaders in our home when they came to visit me. A church had now been established and we held proper Sunday services. It was growing and more people knew about us. I no longer played with other girls who were not Born Again. I was told they would lure me into sin. My days were spent at school and my evenings at prayer services. I would even lead the prayer services with my sermons, but I still found myself feeling more and more confused and alone in my world.

Even after joining the Born Again group, I continued to grow like any other teenager. I was sixteen years old and experiencing all sorts of things that come with being an adolescent. I had already had two or three crushes when I thought I was in love. When I became a Born Again Christian I had to stop seeing those boys because Born Again Christian girls were not allowed to mix with boys unless they were also part of the ministry. Then I developed a crush on someone in my class. He was a few years older than me and his name was Titus. Quiet and new to the school, he was handsome and not like the other boys in the village, the ones who always wanted to make me feel as if they owned me and to whom I had to give in out of peer pressure or because of the fear of being victimised. I had already tried to fancy some of those boys purely because my friends thought a guy was cute or I was terrified of him.

In most cases when we walked back from school, we would find a group of four or five boys waiting for us at some spot to try their luck. Some days they would win, some days we would be saved by those in a passing car or tractor who would offer us a lift. There were two girls who most of the boys in all the villages fancied – Martha and Onicca: they were very light in complexion and considered beautiful. Onicca was an obvious victim because she had come from a township in Johannesburg to live with her uncle. She was an outsider because she spoke a different language. A lot of guys wanted to score with her and many managed to do so.

Apart from being considered beautiful, Martha was the daughter of the principal at one of the schools. She was often victimised because her father was known for his terrifying corporal punishment of the students at his school.

Titus came from another village and was a bit older than the boys who gave the girls a hard time, so I felt differently towards him from the start. I also happened to share a desk with him because when he came to enrol at our school, it was already late in the year and the only available space was at my desk. I believed I was in love with Titus; he seemed very calm and grown up, and he also had something mysterious about him. No one knew him that well but that did not really matter. I at least knew where he lived and that he was in the same class as me. Nothing else was important. In that part of the country, there was no such thing as dating. You were just so-and-so's girlfriend. You either saw each other at school or you waited until an opportunity presented itself, for example, if you were sent to the shops.

Because I lived in a village far away from the one Titus stayed in, no one in our village knew about me having a crush on him. When he started flirting with me, it was exciting and confusing at the same time. Then came the day he told me he loved me. It was in July during study period. We were sitting next to each other and my friend Charlotte was sitting with us. Behind us sat my other friends Sophia, Tshidi, Kgaugelo and Tebogo, who were all busy studying.

When Titus whispered he loved me, Charlotte heard him. She quickly stood up and called Tebogo to come with her to the toilets. Charlotte had a good understanding of what was going on because she had married earlier that year. After Charlotte and Tebogo left the classroom, I told the charming Titus that I liked him as well.

I was overwhelmed. For the first time in my life someone had told me that they loved me. My family was not particularly affectionate or demonstrative – we would only be kissed when my mother was going away or when one of the relatives from far away came to visit. Kissing each other was a sign of love and affection. I was shy when Titus told me that he loved me. I blushed and eagerly waited for the school day to end so that I could share the news with Tebogo.

She was the only one I could confide in because she was a year older than me and she knew how these things felt. On the way home after school, I told her about what had happened in the classroom.

'Oh, I know,' Tebogo said. 'Charlotte told me when she called me to go with her to the toilets. She overheard Titus and she was feeling uncomfortable listening to him so she decided to go outside but she wanted to share the news with someone else.'

Both Tebogo and I were still attending the church although we were no longer as dedicated. By contrast, Charlotte was even more committed to the church since she was now married to one of the pastors. She was acting as a watchdog over Tebogo and me because she felt very strongly about the church and the dangers of converts slipping back into bad habits. According to Tebogo, Charlotte feared I was going to say yes to Titus and she was afraid that her association with the would-be lovers might be frowned on by the rest of the church.

But Tebogo and I thought it was a wonderful thing that a guy like Titus found me attractive and that he was in love with me. We discussed what it would be like when Tebogo also met someone like Titus, which she soon did. We kept each other's secret – our interest in men – and continued to drift away from the church.

After that day, I would flirt with Titus now and again. I told myself that because I was still young and still belonged to the church, even though I was thinking of leaving, I would have to wait to get married. I had already been violated so I knew nothing better. I had no idea that people fall in love and have sex properly. I did not understand how it was done. At church, we were told we had to wait until we were married because 'sex before marriage is a sin'. That provided a good escape for me.

One day at the end of August when we were writing trial examinations, Titus asked me to accompany him to where he stayed because he had forgotten a book. I agreed; unlike other boys, he had not tried to have sex with me. He had never spoken to me about those things and I thought we were platonic lovers and nothing more. So when I went with him to his house, I did not expect anything more than to fetch the book. I was excited to walk with him because the fact that I stayed in a village far from his meant there was never time to see him except for when we were in class and after school before I went home. It was difficult to spend time together.

When we got to the house, he told me the book was in his room, which was at the back of the main house. The room only had a reception area and then the door that led to the bedroom. There was no seating in the reception. We both walked straight into the bedroom. Naive and so trusting, I did not think anything of it. He asked me to sit on the bed while he looked for the book, then suddenly bent down and kissed me – a wonderful thing which I had never experienced from a man before. I did not know how to respond and I told him I had never been kissed before. I asked him what he wanted me to do, and he said, 'I want to have sex with you.'

I told him I could not do that because I was not ready and I would feel uncomfortable. The next thing I knew, he was on top of me telling me he thought I was his girlfriend and that was what boyfriends and girlfriends did.

I could not stand up as he was still on top of me and now pushing my school dress up, now reaching for my underwear. I began to scream, 'Leave me alone! I do not want to sleep with you! I am not ready!'

He was now firmly on top of me and his penis was at the mouth of my vagina. Just as he was about to push inside me, I kicked out and he fell to the floor. I pulled up my underwear and ran out of the room, into the streets and back to school.

I was in a state of shock and disbelief but I had to keep quiet about it when I got to the classroom. Who would I tell? I had asked for it. As I walked into the classroom, everyone looked at me as if they knew what had happened. I had forgotten that my hair was messed up and my school dress was creased and half zipped on the side. I was breathing heavily because I had been running all the way. I sat down and kept my head lowered. I bent down under the desk to hide my embarrassment and to fix my dress. I realised my underwear was wet but thought it did not matter; I had managed not to have sex with him.

Ten minutes later, Titus walked in and went to sit at another desk at the back of the classroom. The boys started whistling as if they knew what had happened. The sounds they made were those of pride and congratulations that he had scored. I was terrified but because I felt I had asked for it, I decided to keep myself together until I could go home. I never told anyone about what had happened, not even Tebogo, and I avoided Titus as much as possible. He never came back to sit with me at our desk.

I began to see my old friends again because I had decided to quit the church. I was no longer feeling the need to seek refuge. It had lost its meaning for me. The prayer meetings, the church services and the Bible studies were all too much and we also went away a lot to preach the gospel at other places. We attended camps and our lives just became a cycle of repetition in our quest for refuge.

Along my Born Again journey I realised something I will never forget. Sometimes while people are trying to avoid certain things in life, they make even more mistakes in their efforts to carry on like normal people. They make bad choices that might even take them back to the very things that they are trying to forget and avoid. If you have never been taught that something is really bad and what its consequences are, you are as doomed as the rest of the people around you. You can call them non-believers or sinners, but underneath it all, you are exactly the same; you simply try a different approach hoping to be better than everybody else.

I knew that in the midst of all my Born Again activity, I was still feeling lonely and empty. I had started having terrible nightmares and my sleeping was not normal. Something was eating me up inside and I felt sick a lot of the time.

Final year exams were approaching. My mouth was always full of saliva, I was almost constantly nauseous and everything started smelling very strange. By the beginning of November, things were getting worse. I had to tell someone about my weird feelings. I had now completely stopped attending church but Tebogo and the other girls were still going so I could not speak to them about my ordeal. I went instead to my friend Dikeledi. She was concerned about me, particularly when I vomited twice while we were talking, and she insisted that I go and see the doctor. So I went to visit Dr Marothi.

'Doctor, I don't know what is wrong with me. For the past three weeks I have been spitting a lot of saliva and everything smells strange. I get terrible headaches but I thought it was because we were writing exams and I was not getting enough rest with all the studying. I also sleep a lot when I am in class. I have to finish my exams.'

'*Wena ngwana wa Mma Modiba.*' ('You, MmaModiba's daughter.') 'I did not know you were naughty. Why have you not been coming back for more pills as I told you last year when you came here with your mother? Look now what you have got yourself into! How is your mother taking all this? I know she is proud of you. I was with her the other day and she told me that you got accepted to go and study at a university in Cape Town. She is proud of you. She did not want you to have a child at such an early age before you finish school, just like your sister and your other three cousins. You have managed to disappoint me. How can you fall pregnant?'

These were Dr Marothi's words after examining me. He had checked me all over and I was already beginning to show. But I had been so caught up in my studying that I thought I was gaining weight because of all the food I was eating. Things had happened so fast I had not even noticed I had missed my periods in September and October.

'But doctor, I don't know what you are talking about, I did not sleep with anyone,' I replied. 'In fact, when the guy I was seeing wanted to sleep with me in September, I kicked him before he could sleep with me. He was about to put his thing inside my vagina when I kicked him. I managed to get up and run away. We are not even on speaking terms now. He avoids me and I don't want anything to do with him.'

Dr Marothi was the son of one of my mother's friends and he knew my family very well. He told me he knew I was not lying,

47

and he asked me to describe exactly how I had pushed the man and when.

'By the time you kicked him, he was already ejaculating so you got his sperm,' explained Dr Marothi. 'I am very sorry this happened. You will have to go to him and tell him this news. You cannot take the responsibility alone.'

Dr Marothi's attempts to explain the technicalities of how a man makes a woman pregnant came very late and they fell on deaf ears for I was in a state of total shock. I was terrified at the thought of how and what I was going to have to do to avoid a terrible punishment from my mother. I had seen her disappointment in Angela when she came home pregnant. Angela was already due when she came home so she had spent all her pregnancy at college without my mother knowing.

'You must have started feeling the slight movements the baby makes. You are far enough along now, it must have started moving. And please, I know you are frightened, but *do not* do anything stupid. There are too many girls who die after discovering they are pregnant. They either commit suicide or they have dangerous abortions where they drink all sorts of mixtures to terminate the pregnancy. You know some of them as well,' said Dr Marothi.

I realised that I had indeed now and again felt the movements in my tummy but I had not known what they were. I begged Dr Marothi not to tell anyone. I promised him I would not do anything stupid, and went straight to Dikeledi's house to share my news. I told Dikeledi how terrified I was and made her promise not to tell anyone. She knew what my mother would do to me so we started plotting to save me. We decided I should talk to Titus and see what he had to say. Maybe he would agree to his share of the responsibility and that would make it easier for me. Then I would not have to tell my mother since in cases when the boy was really in love with the girl, his parents would go to the girl's parents to apologise on his behalf and offer some form of compensation. However, that was if the two had had sex properly. I was confused.

On my way home, I agonised over the thought of having a baby myself and over what my mother would do to me. I considered myself too young to have a baby. I had big dreams for myself and was about to go to university. I had helped to look after my sister's baby so I knew what babies did and I was not sure I could handle a child that had not been conceived with my consent. Now I had a difficult task ahead of me; I was supposed to tell Titus. I did not know how he was going to react since we had not spoken since I kicked him. We were writing exams and it was unlikely we would bump into each other because the matriculants were scattered all over the schools due to a lack of space at our school. Titus and I were not writing at the same centre.

I thought I would look like a fool trying to explain to him how the doctor believed it had happened. Maybe I should simply walk up to him and say: 'That day when you tried to force me to sleep with you, you made me pregnant.' But I did not want to embarrass myself. I also did not want other people to know I was pregnant and how it had happened. I blamed myself for everything.

It was late November and everyone was attending the wedding of the very same doctor who had told me I was pregnant. I saw Titus and his cousin at the wedding. Feeling very brave, I went to them and told him I needed to speak to him. He was friendly and calm as usual and did not make a scene. He looked happy that I was talking to him, suspecting nothing, and he told me we could speak after the wedding.

Later we sat in his cousin's car so we could talk in private.

'I have been sick for a long time now and I went to see the doctor,' I said after a long moment of silence.

'Oh, what is the problem?' he asked.

'Dr Marothi told me that I am pregnant.'

49

Now I was regretting that I had started the conversation. I felt shy and stupid.

'*Ijo, o re o imesitswe ke mang?*' Titus asked. ('Who did he say is the father?')

'It's you, he said. On the day we went to fetch your book together,' I replied, shocked at the question.

'It definitely was not me. I have never slept with you. You kicked me remember? And besides, I do not want to talk about it. I don't know what to say to you but it surely was not my doing,' he said with annoyance in his voice.

Now even more disappointed and confused, I tried to explain to Titus how the doctor said it could have happened but he dismissed me, telling me he was tired.

I got out of the car and left without saying anything more. I felt the tears roll down my cheeks but I also felt brave as I realised I would have to save myself from the situation. I was even more terrified of my mother's reaction now that I had no one to share the responsibility with me. The following day I went to Dikeledi to tell her what had happened. I told her we would have to find a way of getting rid of the pregnancy before my mother found out.

'And you are really beginning to show now,' Dikeledi warned. 'You must find a solution fast. I have heard of this girl who had an abortion and maybe we should go and ask her where she had it done. But you know that a lot of girls have died while aborting. You remember your cousin Pinky who died earlier in the year? What are you going to do now?'

'I think we must go and find out from this girl what she did and where. I don't want my mother to kill me. Besides, I want to go to university in January,' I answered tearfully.

The two of us were naive and inexperienced. We had no knowledge about how far along you should be to terminate a pregnancy and what mental and physical scars you would carry with you after terminating a pregnancy. We knew nothing about preabortion counselling or counselling in general. Dikeledi had the task of finding the other girl and getting the information from her.

A few days later we had our answer. We were told there were places in town that helped girls to terminate their pregnancies and we had one address. Now the dilemma was that we had no money with which to travel to town. Dikeledi borrowed money from a friend and we both went to town to find the place. It looked like a doctor's surgery in an area called the Indian Centre. We found two ladies with unpleasant faces. Maybe it was because of the nature of the work they performed that they no longer found joy in life. They looked very serious and manipulative.

'How can we be of help to you girls?' The ladies both asked us at the same time.

'We came to ask if you could help. I am pregnant,' I said.

The women looked at each other.

'Yes, we can help and the fee is R450,' the older lady said. 'You cannot tell anyone though. It has to remain a secret that you came here. Our doctor might or might not be here on the day that we perform the procedure. If you have the money, you can have it done now and go home. It is quick.'

The woman had a funny face with lots of pigmentation that made her look even more serious than the other one who was young and very pretty. They did not ask how far along I was. We told them we did not have the money with us. We agreed that we would go and get the money and return another day.

Dikeledi and I had never heard of a 'backstreet abortion'. At that time, abortion was still illegal. We knew very little about it, how it was performed and who should perform it. Our only mission was to save me from my predicament. We said our goodbyes and left the place. On our way home we started thinking of ways to get hold of R450. I knew I could not ask my mother. But I quickly thought of someone who might be willing to help and keep the secret as well.

51

At this time, the exams were finished and everybody was preparing for the festive season. There was a man who was interested in me and had been pursuing me for a while. He seemed very serious about me because he did not rush me to make a decision. He was already working so he had money. Dikeledi suggested I should ask him for the money.

I told him the whole truth and he offered to help. He told me he would bring R300 the following day but since he was going away for a few days, he could only give me the rest of the money when he got back. He was very understanding. Then Dikeledi and I went back to the ladies and begged them to help us. We said we would bring the balance once the job was done.

The ladies did not have a problem with this arrangement but I had a problem with the so-called 'procedure'. I was not at all prepared for what was about to happen. They were going to insert a metal instrument inside my vagina to perform the procedure and I was terrified of it. I had never seen a speculum before because I had never had a gynaecological check-up. I was so frightened of the instrument that I refused to have the procedure.

One of the ladies muttered, 'Stop behaving like a young child. Girls your age and those even younger than you never give us problems. So, what is your problem?'

Dikeledi was terrified as well. But she had to be calm in order to convince me to go through with it and let the ladies do their work. They told me that they used the instrument to open the womb and make sure the baby came out as if I was having a miscarriage. They did not care how far along I was.

I still refused to let them insert the instrument inside me and stormed out of the rooms, leaving behind the R300 I had already paid. Dikeledi came after me and tried to talk me into going back. At this point, I did not care what happened to the R300. I was terrified. In the taxi on our way home, I was crying and all the time I thought of running away instead of facing those two ladies and their instrument. Dikeledi comforted me and assured me that when we went back, it would not be so scary now that I had seen the instrument and had time to think about it.

'You have to think of your mother and what she will do to you. Also, remember you have already paid R300, and what are you going to tell the person who gave you the money? It will be okay. We will go back tomorrow.'

Dikeledi was trying to be brave. She could see I was terrified. More than anything, I was scared of the unknown. I had not been given enough information about the process. The ladies needed the money, and I needed to get rid of my problem. I thought about it and realised I might as well do it and go to my grave with the secret. I couldn't bear having to face my mother. I knew our plan was still the best and committed myself to going back the next day.

It was too late. My mother was beginning to suspect something was wrong with me. My behaviour was abnormal. I was always sad; I refused to eat and did not want to sit with the rest of the family any more. The next day as I was walking out of the house, unaware that my mother was walking right behind me, I spat a blob of saliva onto the ground. As I tried to cover it with soil, my mother snapped at me and demanded to know exactly what was going on. I was told to get back to the house and go to my bed-room. I began to cry.

'What is happening to you? Is there something wrong in your body or is it just my imagination? Are you pregnant? If you are, who is the father and is he going to marry you?'

I nodded and told my mother the doctor had said I was sick. She asked so many questions at once that I didn't have a chance to tell her everything. I was struggling to keep up with her anger and shock.

'What is he saying? Will he marry you? Because I will not be taking care of yet another baby in my house without a father!'

53

It was all too much and I began to throw up on the bed. During our confrontation, my mother told me that if I was really pregnant it was the end of me. I must forget about my studies and about going to Cape Town. By now the Matric results were out and in spite of how sick I had felt I had passed very well with a university exemption. I was due to leave for Cape Town at the beginning of January. Now I would have to stay at home and take care of the baby. My mother did not ask me how it had happened, she simply assumed I was in a sexual relationship. This seemed to make sense to her because I had arrived home very late one night (the night I had told Titus I was pregnant) and had been given a good hiding. I also remembered that hiding, and remembered I was beaten up so badly that I had vowed not to say anything to my mother because she would kill me if she knew the whole story and about the pregnancy.

I cried while my mother shook me and demanded answers. I told my mother Titus's name and that he was not going to marry me. I told her I was going to terminate the pregnancy and said I had already paid a sum of money.

What was coming out of my mouth paralysed my mother. She was no longer looking at her little girl on the blue train. I shocked myself as well; there I was sitting in my own bedroom telling my mother I was going to have an abortion. I did not know what else she wanted me to say. She asked me where I had got the money from and who was going to do the termination. The horror grew even worse because she stormed out of the room without waiting for my answers or telling me what she was thinking.

After she left, I ran to Dikeledi to tell her what I had just been through. We had to find the balance of the money and go back to town immediately. Dikeledi suggested a friend of hers as a source for the rest of the money. I could repay her when the man who had given me the R300 returned from his trip.

I do not know if Dikeledi told her friend what the money was for as I waited outside the house while they spoke. We went straight from there back to town to those ladies. When we arrived at the door, Dikeledi did not go with me into the treatment room where the procedure was performed. This time, although I was frightened, my mother's reaction had given me courage. I realised what was at stake – my life, my future and my mother's peace of mind.

I lay there in agony and screamed as they performed the procedure on me. I knew I had to go through with it and tried not to think of those other girls who had died. I wanted to save my life. My screaming did not bother anyone. No one showed any remorse for what was happening and I was told to go home as soon as they had finished.

'The rest will happen naturally,' the women told me and there was no further explanation. I paid the R150 and we left. Dikeledi put her arm around me as we went to the taxis.

When I got home I went straight to my room to hide. Before I knew it, I began to have what felt like period pains. Unaware of what to expect or how to ask for help, I locked my bedroom door and cried alone. Later, around midnight, probably because she could not sleep, my mother came to get answers to her questions and could not get into my room as it was locked. She shouted at me to open the door. I was in such pain but I knew I had to open the door. I crawled on the floor to open the door. I was sobbing in terrible pain. Water had just come out of my genitals. My mother could no longer get her answers. She was scared by what she was seeing. She must have thought I was dying.

She asked Sipho to call my aunt to come and help her. When my aunt got there, they decided to rush me to the health centre. All the way there, I was screaming in pain, 'Ma, I am dying, this thing is painful! I am dying, please help me push!'

I felt an urge to push; I was kicking and screaming. My mother and aunt had to hold me and they prayed I would not die before we got to the health centre. They were both frightened and trying to calm me down but nothing was helping. I was now in more pain than ever before. I thought I was about to die.

'I need to push mommy and it hurts,' I kept screaming. My aunt held me in her arms while my mother rubbed my feet. The guy driving us was my mother's uncle and he did not want to ask too many questions. When we reached the health centre, everything was ready to come out. The nurses at the emergency door brought a stretcher and rushed me to the emergency room.

'Wena ngwanenyana,' ('You, young girl') 'you are sixteen to seventeen weeks pregnant. But you are in labour and you have already dilated. We need to take you inside the delivery room,' one of the nurses said as she checked me after my arrival to the emergency room. But she was too late. Immediately after they examined me, I pushed and it was there. Something dropped out of my body onto the floor.

'Mmawee, mmawee,' ('Mommy, Mommy') 'please help, this thing is going to bite me – it even has a tail!'

That was me screaming for help. I was frightened that the thing I saw lying on the floor next to me which had come out of my vagina was a small dog that was going to bite me. In shock, I had no idea what I thought I was seeing. I didn't know what to expect but I was so frightened by what came out of my body with so much pain that I was not ready to deal with another pain of being bitten by that thing. I was in a deranged state. I was shocked by the fact that its tail was attached to me and I could not move without it moving with me. I screamed for help again. The two nurses who were in the room with me just whispered amongst themselves. My mother and aunt waited outside.

Now, lying on the floor, the scary thing that might bite me was having its tail cut off by the two nurses.

The nurses went outside to tell my mother and aunt that I had been pregnant but had already aborted. My mother and aunt came into the room. They just looked at me; they did not know what to say. There it was, lying on the floor, an almost seventeen-week-old male fetus. I could see its genitals and the heart beating, and I watched it as life left it after the cord was cut by one of the nurses.

I was admitted into the health centre's ward. I had no idea what had happened to the fetus. My body was too exhausted for me even to think and I was bleeding terribly. The nurses in the ward told me to go to the bathroom and clean myself up.

The following morning, Dr Marothi, who was the only doctor in the area, came to check on new patients. He found me lying there and looked at my file with shock. 'I thought I told you not to do anything stupid. You could have died. Anyway, let's see how you are doing.' He did not say much more. He did his job and left.

My mother and aunt came to visit in the morning. They brought me food and told me they had to take care of 'the parcel'. During the day Moyahabo came to visit. She saw what was written in the file – 'Abortion' – but made no comment.

I was now thinking of the pain I had gone through and how I had managed to survive. It was becoming real to me that I could have died. My cousin Pinky had died earlier in the year after having an abortion. She was found a week later in the house in which she stayed alone since her mother worked far away from home. Her body had turned green. One of her cousins found her after not seeing her at school for a long time. When I was in such pain, I had kept seeing images of Pinky as well as of my great-grandmother who had also passed on. I had thought they were welcoming me to the other side. I could not believe my luck when I found I was still alive.

I was soon discharged from the health centre. When I arrived home, I discovered it was my cousin's twenty-first birthday and everyone had gone to her party. I was left alone in the house.

Then, fortunately, Dikeledi came to visit and we talked about how relieved we both were that I was alive.

I was traumatised and alone. Nothing at all about my ordeal was mentioned at home. I thought that maybe if I had died during the experience, people would have felt sorry for me. Other girls died, and they were buried and life went on. People gossiped about their deaths. Two weeks later I packed and left for university in the Western Cape. I disappeared into the world of Cape Town where no one knew who I was, and that suited me very well.

5

My mother took me to the airport so that I could catch my flight to Cape Town. It was the first time I had flown, although I had been to the airport before when my mother went overseas, and had seen aeroplanes up close on a school trip to a nearby Air Force base. This time around I was going to be in the aeroplane myself.

Matome had been a very loving big brother. He had taken me on a shopping spree and for the first time in my life I was able to choose my own clothes. In the past, my mother had always bought new clothes for me. She would make sure Angela and I were wearing matching clothes on Christmas and New Year's Day, both traditionally times when parents bought their children new clothes. Most children in the village dressed very smartly on Christmas Day.

Apart from that, new clothes meant new school uniforms, which were a must. Girls would wear a long dress for years because their parents did not want to buy a new one every year. My mother also made us clothes on her own machine. Fashion trends were not an issue; clothing meant one's body was covered.

I was very excited when Matome took me to town to buy new clothes. He had good taste and he and Sipho always looked stylish because Matome took care of the male clothing department in our house. Angela and I were usually at our mother's mercy. She always bought us large sizes so we could grow into the clothes. Since I had been a Born Again Christian for a while, I had no long pants, for we were not allowed to wear any trousers; neither were we permitted earrings, fashionable hair styles or short skirts. My wardrobe was full of long skirts and ethnic dresses. Matome had been exposed to College life and he suggested we buy jeans, takkies, pants and blouses. It was a wonderful experience for me.

Everyone at home knew that I was leaving for Cape Town – my friends, my schoolteachers and my relatives. It was a milestone, and not just for me: I was the first girl in my village to go and study in Cape Town. My grandmother spoke to the ancestors on my behalf to make sure they would take care of me while I was away from home. Angela baked cookies for me and my mother packed my suitcases. I was given a bank card so the family could send me money easily. Matome had promised to make sure I received pocket money from him.

Before I left, 'Mr Money', the man who had paid for my abortion, came to see me. He was very proud of me and of the fact that I was leaving to go to university. He had given me the balance of the money so that Dikeledi could pay back her friend. He and Dikeledi were the only ones who seemed to care about what had happened two weeks previously. We said our goodbyes and my mother and I caught a bus to Johannesburg. Sipho was not at home to say goodbye to me because he had disappeared two weeks before I left. He had failed his Matric again and wanted to go out into the world and experiment. He was now a grown man who rebelled against the rules.

'You must not be scared of the airplane. You just need to relax when you take off and before you know it you will be landing. You must take good care of yourself when you get to the university. You can call and write any time,' my mother assured me before I got on to the plane.

Cape Town seemed like another world to me, a strange place with strange people and buildings. I had always told my friends at school that when I grew up I was going to study overseas. Indeed, Cape Town *was* overseas to me. The people back at home believed that I was going overseas; most of them did not know the difference. The fact that there was a sea in Cape Town made it overseas. I worried that I would be completely lost and that I did not belong there.

I had to share a room with someone since all the first-year students stayed in double rooms. I arrived early so my room-mate Dipuo found me settled into our room already. We clicked immediately because her family was from my region and she knew my language.

Something that I initially found difficult was the wide use of English. Apart from when I had been debating, I had not conversed in English before and it was hard to cope with the English-speaking lecturers and students. Even the people who at least looked like me also spoke languages I had never heard before – Xhosa, Tswana, Zulu and South Sotho. I only knew about Venda and Tsonga because they were spoken closer to where I come from. I kept quiet a lot because I had nothing to say. This made me feel even more isolated and lonely. In the beginning I desperately wanted to go back home to my familiar environment.

Then there was the food in the dining hall to cope with. One day the menu read: 'Monkey Gland steak'.

'Monkey? I am not going to eat monkey meat,' I told the girls as we went into the dining hall. 'I would rather have only bread and juice.'

I might have eaten locusts and other insects which we caught to eat back home – *masonja* (mopani worms), *dintlwamakhura* (small black flying insects) and *dinonyana* (birds) – but I was not prepared to eat monkey meat. Even when someone explained to me that 'Monkey Gland' was only a kind of sauce, I was still not convinced.

It was orientation week and we were shown around the campus, the lecture halls, student centre, library and study halls. We also had to register and choose courses. I was disappointed that I could not enrol for a degree that would allow me to become a Chartered Accountant because I had not passed Mathematics in my Matric. Instead, I opted for a degree that still allowed me to study Accountancy and Business Economics. I was also introduced to the world of Industrial Psychology, Political Studies, Mercantile Law and Public Management. All of the subjects involved putting together long and well-researched assignments. They also meant engaging in a lot of debate in the lecture halls and during the tutorial classes.

It was almost impossible for me to communicate with my friends back home because Tebogo, Sharlotte and Dikeledi did not have telephones. I wrote them letters. I wanted them to know I was missing them. The letters would take a month to reach my friends because they were sent to the school, and the principal would have to sort out the post and distribute it during assembly. Then it would take a long time before I received their replies.

'Kedibone, Room 8, phone call,' called one of the girls from the corridor. My first phone call was from my mother who wanted to know how I was and to tell me I could always do a reverse charges call home. The following day I got a call from 'Mr Money'. He had asked Dikeledi for my number and wanted me to know he still wanted me to be his girlfriend. He had even sent me a letter and asked if I had received it yet.

On the 14th of February, Valentine's Day, I received a gift and a beautiful card from 'Mr Money'. I was confused but excited by the attention. At least someone thought I was special. The question was, could I make another person feel special? I had my own problems – getting lost around the campus, trying to make friends, getting involved in my studies.

Although I found it hard to make friends, I did manage to meet some girls from the same province as myself, which helped me to feel a little more settled. One of my new friends, Gladys, even offered to take me out to town, saying we could eat a pizza.

'*Pitsa*?' I thought, and told Gladys, 'I'm sorry but I can't eat a *pitsa*.' The word 'pizza' sounds like *pitsa*, which in my language means a pot. Since I had never seen or heard of a pizza before, I was shocked when she told me we were going to a pizza place. It was obvious I was not going to eat something I associated with metal. Anyway, I refused to taste it and stuck to a burger.

I still cried a lot every time I was alone. I wanted so badly to go back home but knew there was no point because I was unhappy there too. In any case, I had to stay and finish my degree. I did not want to fail and go home a loser and I had come too far to disappoint myself. I was desperate to succeed, and for that success not to be associated with my life back home. To succeed there meant you had to beat the odds. The issues involved in beating the odds were not just simple or normal day-to-day ones, but difficult ones; only the fit survived. I learned from my mother when I phoned that my friend Dalia had committed suicide. In that part of the world everything bad – nightmares, accidents, illnesses, sufferings, misfortune – were a result of bad luck or, even worse, curses from your ancestors or witchcraft. You died because someone bewitched you. You got sick because the ancestors were angry with you. You had bad luck because your ancestors were not happy with you. You failed at school because you were stupid and you had no intelligent genes.

Nothing was ever said about making mistakes or making bad choices. What could a girl like me know about bad choices? And what about things over which you had no control? No one ever chose to be affected by environment and circumstances; it was simply life and it happened.

I was battling to sleep at night. If I did fall asleep, I had nightmares and night terrors. I thought I was being suffocated. One day Dipuo asked me why I was looking sad and tired.

'I don't really sleep well at night,' was all I could say to her. I thought to myself that Dipuo would not understand. In any case, I had had no practice at being vocal about issues. I was used to a culture of secrecy and silence. People tend to fend for themselves when they are faced with serious issues such as poverty, malnutrition, lack of facilities, poor education, unemployment, and single mothers bringing up children with little or no income. The society and community believe that a lot of things are taboo. I suffered alone in silence. I could not talk to my room-mate or to my new friends, Nomsa, Maria and Nthabiseng, about my background. I was not able to be free with them.

I was getting into a routine: study, dining hall, laundry, meeting with friends here and there, writing in my journal and sleeping. I continued to write letters to my friends back home but their replies became less frequent. They had nothing in common with me any more. I was in another world, a world they could not get to. They were struggling to pass their Matric, and those who had passed were struggling to get finance to further their studies. Some were being sold into marriages with men old enough to be their fathers by their parents because they needed to lessen the family's financial burden.

One day I received a letter. Dikeledi wrote:

Dear Kedibone,

It is nice to write you a letter. School is fine and I hope to pass Matric this year. So many things have happened since you left. Mmabatho's mother got her married because she

*owed the guy some money and she could not pay him back.
The man wanted her daughter in return. She is married, my
friend. She is now in Venda with her husband. Margaret had
a baby boy, the father refused to accept the responsibility, she
now works at the farms. Remember those trucks that used to
come in the morning to fetch ladies so that they could work in
the fields in exchange for potatoes and tomatoes? She is now
one of those ladies, my friend. Onicca died from abortion.
That reminded me of you. We will be going to the funeral
this weekend. The teachers have asked us to prepare an item
to sing at the funeral. Your mother must have told you about
Tinti's suicide a few weeks ago. By the way, your brother,
Sipho, made some girl pregnant. I am sure by the time you
get home, the child will be born. 'Mr Money' always asks me
about you. He really loves you, my friend. At least he is
educated and he can speak English. I think you should get
serious about him. Maybe the two of you will get married
one day. He is one of the rare ones. I myself am trying to
find someone like him. Your Born Again Christian friends
have stopped going to church. I guess they finally realised
that we are all sinners.*

*I hope you are showing them what you are made of down
there in Cape Town. I hope I will pass my Matric this year.*

*Regards,
Dikeledi*

I cried for hours after reading her letter. Dikeledi had inserted a
picture of herself in her school uniform. She was now almost a
grown woman and in a way she was speaking up. She was my
pillar of strength and she wanted to see me happy.

That evening, I took Dikeledi's advice and wrote a short letter
to 'Mr Money':

Dear Paul,

Thank you so much for the Valentine gift and the beautiful card you sent me. It really made me feel special. I am trying to be a good girl down here. I so wish I had spent more time with you when I was still at home. And to think, I never thanked you enough for the money you gave me. You took the responsibility for something that had nothing to do with you. I hope to see you very soon. I think I should love you, well I do love you.

Regards,
Kedibone

I had doubts writing the words 'I do love you'. I knew nothing about love and wondered if I could truly love anyone. I confused gratitude with love. At the same time, I found myself becoming strongly attracted to men. I knew there was Paul back home but because I did not know what love was, I wanted to experiment. I hit on the first man I thought was cute although he had no real interest in me. He was my Political Science tutor and was calm and handsome, similar to Titus in many ways. I wanted to experiment with sex. This time around at least I would be the one playing the game. This is not to say I planned his seduction; it was more as if I let myself be guided by my confusion. I wanted to feel loved. So I started flirting with my tutor to get his attention.

And it worked. The affair only lasted for two months until I realised that all he did was get drunk and come to my room for sex. It made me feel cheap and I could not take it any more. Paul was getting serious about me; he wanted me to finish studying so that he could marry me. I knew I did not love him but I continued to lead him on.

Immediately after I broke it off with my tutor, I met Alan who was from the same province as me. What I had with Alan was probably my first real experience of falling in love but I had no concept of what it meant to love and be loved by a man. Although our relationship was to last for five and a half years, I did not reciprocate Alan's love. I could not be content with what we had and tended to view him as a brother and not a boyfriend.

I continued to communicate with Paul and the first time I went home for the holidays, I spent time with him. One day while walking in the village, I saw Titus. The two of us sat down and talked for an hour. I wanted him to acknowledge what he had done to me – at least to accept that the aborted child was his and to be willing to make up for his mistakes. I asked him to be my boyfriend and this time I told myself I would be able to get back at him and control him, punish him for what he had done. He did not think it was a good idea but I was persistent.

'I know you love me. You are just angry with me for refusing to have sex with you,' I told him.

Titus wanted to know what had happened to the pregnancy and I told him what I had done. I had no feelings about the whole thing. All I wanted was for him to acknowledge me but it was clear the two of us would never become an item. I was going back to Cape Town and any relationship between us would be a long-distance one. When Titus finally agreed to keep in touch with me, I thought I had got him.

I would see Paul sometimes, meet up with Alan, and visit Titus at his home. None of them was aware of my other involvements. I never had sex with Titus but I slept with both Paul and Alan even though I did not reciprocate their love. Time after time I distanced myself from both of them and tried to have fun with other men. At one point Paul even drove down to Cape Town to find out why I was ignoring him, not taking his calls or writing back to him. I thought I could protect myself from loss and abandonment by running away and being promiscuous. I was on a man-hurting spree.

6

During the June/July holidays, I visited my Aunt Thabitha for a week. One morning when I woke up I overheard her talking about me with one of the ladies who worked for her. My aunt had no idea I could hear the conversation.

'It seems like the little madam here is suffering from *bolwetsi bja go wa*,' whispered my aunt, meaning, 'She is suffering from a disease which makes her pass out' (epilepsy, in other words).

At the time, I did not know what my problem was. All I knew was I had woken up on the floor and must have fallen out of bed. I was wet and my tongue was terribly bitten and swollen. I had no idea what had happened to me. But I knew what my aunt meant by *bolwetsi bja go wa*.

I knew that many people in our community suffered from the condition. I had learned that it was something that was either related to poverty or that happened to you when your ancestors were trying to communicate with you. The thought of having *bolwetsi bja go wa* was frightening because I remembered clearly that when I was at school, we used to laugh at other children who would pass out during the morning devotions at assembly. One day a girl nearly fell on me but I ducked, and my friends and I laughed at her. I knew the stigma that came with *bolwetsi bja go wa*. How could I be one of them?

Though I had wet my bed until I was in Standard Nine, it had not happened since and I could not believe it was starting again. This time around I thought that maybe I had had a bad dream and I was very embarrassed about it. As for my swollen tongue, I thought I must have bitten it as I fell.

My aunt never said anything to me about it and when she dropped me off at home she did not mention the incident to my mother. I also thought nothing more about it until a week later when I woke up to find that I had wet the bed again. This time my mother walked into the room to find me looking at the wet sheets.

'Why would you still wet your bed at your age? Are you sick?' my mother asked.

'I don't know. I think I had a bad dream,' I answered, extremely embarrassed. I had never been close to my mother and recent months had not improved our relationship, so our conversations were always short and to the point. I was still terrified of her interrogations.

I could not connect this incident to what had occurred at my aunt's house. To me, there was nothing new about my bed-wetting. Since I had done it for a long time while I was living at home, it could be that I was having a relapse. I told my mother it was a bad dream and because of the heat, I must have sweated a lot. The incident was never discussed and I went back to university.

Nothing further happened until a Thursday towards the end of the year. It was two days before the university was due to close for the December holidays. I had finished writing my main exams and was scheduled to write a medical exam for one subject I had been unable to write on the actual date because I had been sick. The medical exam was on a Friday afternoon and I was catching a bus in the evening to go home. Everything was planned such that when I finished writing I would leave for the bus station.

I had already packed my things and was spending the night in Alan's room.

'Ma'am, do you know if you are perhaps pregnant?' the lady in a white dress asked me. I thought I was dreaming, finding myself lying in a strange bed. I did not know where I was or how I had got there. The lady saw my confusion and spoke again: 'Ma'am, you are in Tygerberg Hospital and I am Nurse Steenkamp. You came here last night from the campus. How are you feeling?'

Coming out of what seemed like a deep sleep, I did not know how I felt. There was nothing attached to me. I was not in any pain.

Alan was sitting on the other side of the bed. I looked at him and wondered why he was there. I did remember that I had been spending the night in his room. If this is a bad dream, then Alan is in it, I thought to myself. My tongue was swollen and I could not understand why I was not wearing my clothes.

'Kedibone, you gave me such a fright last night,' Alan said. 'I thought you were going to die. I had to call the matron to help me get an ambulance so that we could bring you here. How are you doing?'

Confused, I started crying. Seeing Alan looking so worried made me cry even more. He looked terrified.

'But why are we in hospital?' I asked.

'Don't you remember what happened at all? You passed out,' Alan replied.

I tried very hard to recall the last time I was awake. The thing I remembered doing was preparing for the medical exam in Alan's room. I had started getting hot flushes and asked Alan to open the windows because I was feeling very hot. The next minute I was very cold. Alan had to open, close and open the windows. I was feeling feverish. And now I was in hospital with no pain at all.

According to Alan, I did fall asleep eventually after all my struggles with fever. Then I woke up in the night trembling and shivering. I had wet the bed and was struggling to speak. I started biting my tongue and fell out of the bed. Alan had tried to hold me so that I did not hurt myself but I passed out.

'You had one of those ancestral attacks,' Alan suggested. He was from the same cultural and ethnic group as me, so he had more or less the same understanding and definition of things as I did.

He had gone to call the resident matron to get an ambulance so that they could take me to the hospital. But the matron suggested they get the campus car to drive me. He had not been sure if he would still find me alive when he arrived back at the room with the matron.

The nurse told me that the doctors at the hospital did not know exactly what was wrong with me and so they wanted to run some tests to determine the cause of my collapse. I refused because I was not in any pain at all and I wanted to get back for my medical exam. I did not understand how the tests would help me. Besides, apart from my time spent at the health centre after the abortion, I did not recall ever being in hospital. Back at home, most of the treatments for my ailments were done by the old ladies. Even on those occasions when I had measles and mumps, my treatments were undertaken either at home or in the fields.

With the mumps, I had to go to an old lady's house so that I could put my head into a *moeta* (a calabash) and shout '*mauwe, mauwe, boela nkgong*' ('mumps, mumps, please return to the calabash where you come from'). A few days later, I was well. For the measles, I had to go to the fields with a male cousin and my mother. There my cousin had to urinate on a *seolo* (soil that has formed a small hill) and then smear the soil wet from his urine all over my naked body, instructing the measles to leave my body and remain in the fields. When we finished, my body was covered with a blanket and we were told not to talk or look back all the way home. Otherwise, the disease would follow me and come back. I had to go straight to bed and not bath until the following morning. All of this was done before sunset and I was well a few days later.

Up to this point in my life I had had no medical tests and I could not understand the need for them. Alan had also frightened me with his 'ancestral attacks' comment. I was fearful of what was going to happen to me. I knew there was no treatment for things related to the ancestors; tests would not reveal anything.

I was discharged from the hospital without any tests being done. Back at the university, I insisted on writing my exam straight away even though I was still confused and did not remember much. When the results came out my poor performance meant that I had failed the Accountancy course that was my only hope of getting closer to my dream of becoming a Chartered Accountant.

Afterwards I went back to my room to find that Alan had already packed my wet clothes in plastic bags. Dipuo was surprised to see me. She said Alan had come to the room looking for my personal things. He had not told her much, only that I was in hospital. The bus was leaving in the evening so I had to make arrangements to get to the bus station. Alan left before me because his bus was an earlier one. He really loved me dearly, I thought to myself as I remembered his reaction at the hospital when I woke up.

'I thought I was going to lose you,' he said.

To me, Alan was the loving and caring brother I had dreamed about but never had. He and Sipho were the same age and Alan and I often behaved more like siblings than a couple. My feelings for him did not go beyond this.

When I got home, my mother was waiting at the bus station because the matron had phoned her, as was university policy, to let her know of my condition and my admission to hospital. My mother was worried about me. I was tired and disorientated. She quickly got hold of our family doctor who referred us to a specialist. For the whole of the next day, my mother and I waited in the doctor's room while tests and scans were run and X-rays taken. Dr Visagie, the physician, called his colleagues to come and help him get to the bottom of the problem.

Later in the evening they found what was causing my seizures: the CAT scan showed that I had a cavity within my brain. For the moment the cause was unknown but I was immediately admitted to a hospital ward and for the next two weeks I was placed under observation. Those two weeks were the scariest of my life. I was inundated with painful tests, among them a lumbar puncture, to determine the source of the cavity and eventually a diagnosis of tuberculosis (TB) was made. When I was finally discharged, the doctors prescribed medication that they told me I would have to take until the hole had healed and the TB was cured, possibly for the rest of my life.

I started calling on the Saviour from whom I had run away to come and save me. I knew I could not be a Born Again Christian any more but I did pray. I prayed for a miracle. I understood the real meaning of the prayer that was taught at primary school level, the prayer I had known from an early age: '*Modimo mpopele pelo ye sekileng, busha o nnele moya wa go tia teng gaka.*' ('Lord, grant me a pure heart, once again grant me a strong inner spirit.')

I also prayed from Psalm 24: 'He who has a clean hand and a pure heart, who does not lift up his soul to what is false, and does not swear deceitfully, he will receive blessings from the Lord and vindication from the God of his salvation.'

These were the prayers I had been taught at Sunday school and at home. I had always carried these prayers with me and now that I was filled with fear again, I turned to them. This time, it was the fear of having to live on TB tablets or of dying from TB. I had to get used to the tablets and make them part of my life, however long that life might be.

I took the news of my condition as a punishment for my having had an abortion and for all the things I had done wrong in my life. In my attempt to better myself, I studied even harder. I was one of the best students. Others came to me to get help with their assignments. I was good at gathering information; all my energies were channelled towards building a detailed knowledge base to beat others. At night I was exhausted. I suffered from insomnia and when I was able to sleep I continued to have nightmares. I became sick and was forever visiting the GP or gynaecologist because I had pains.

Alan was very patient with me, even though he knew by now that I did not feel the same way about him as he felt about me. I was slowly withdrawing from him. Paul had been dumped along the way. He did not even get a proper goodbye.

7

It was my second year at university and Alan and I were still together – just. We had fights like any other couple, but the most recent one had got completely out of hand.

'Tell me about your life back at home, about your parents and the rest of the family,' said the woman sitting across from me on the couch.

'There is nothing much to tell; I am just upset. My boyfriend hurt me very much.' I was resisting the conversation. I had been sent to the Student Counselling Centre by the campus nurse. I knew nothing about counselling. I had only heard of it recently while doing an Industrial Psychology Course, the first part of which was Behavioural Psychology.

I was wondering why the campus nurse would send me to Student Counselling because I had fought with my boyfriend. I had to admit that it had not been an ordinary fight. I had nearly killed Alan. He was taken to the hospital to be stitched up after I nearly cut his throat with a knife. I was very upset.

It had happened the night before: I had wanted to kill Alan. I had gone to his room and found him opening a can of beans with a knife. I grabbed the knife away from him and that was how it all started.

'I will kill you. I am going to kill you. I want to kill you!' I cried as I tried to stick the knife into Alan's throat. When he managed to take the knife from me, I reached for a glass and broke it on the window sill.

Alan tried to calm me down but I was far too upset. Nothing he did or said could stop my rage. He had never seen me like that; no one had ever seen me like that – not my mother, my siblings or my friends. I acted as if I was possessed.

Alan was terrified. I had so much strength that he was struggling to keep me on the floor. As I was trying to stab him, the only thought in my mind was that no man would ever hurt me again and get away with it. Alan kept apologising and begging me to stop before I hurt him. 'I am so sorry, Kedibone. I did not mean to hurt you. Can we please talk about this in a calm way? Put the knife down, Kedibone, you are going to hurt us both.'

'Hurt? Who said I want to hurt you? You are the one who hurt *me*! I came here to kill you! Today is your last day alive!'

The more Alan tried to calm me down, the more dangerous I became. I was no longer talking to him; I was seeing images.

A friend of Alan's opened the door but did not grasp the situation. He said: 'Oh, you two are playing with knives now?'

'No, Simon, this woman is going to kill me; you have to help me calm her down. She is behaving very strangely,' Alan begged his friend.

'If you guys are seriously fighting, then I'd better go and call the campus police.'

Simon left the room. I was now getting weak and confused as to what was happening. It was like the devil that had possessed me was leaving my body. I was out of breath and sobbing but Alan was hurt and bleeding. I had managed to cut him with the broken glass after he had taken the knife away from me. The stabbing was not strategic or that of someone who knew how to fight. The person fighting Alan was not an adult but a little girl.

I left Alan in his room and went back to my own. When Simon returned with the campus police, I was gone. Suzan, my second-year room-mate, wondered what had happened. She had seen me before I left to go to Alan's room and I had told her I was going to kill him, but she had not thought I was serious. She knew I was very upset with Alan.

During the day, I had confronted a girl with whom Alan was having an affair. The affair had been going on for three months right under my nose. I had long stopped being intimate with Alan and had told him I was not sure if I really loved him. He was very patient with me, suffered my mood swings and did not pressure me at all. I had once asked him to break up with me but I went back to him almost immediately. He just let me be.

I did not recognise that there was anything wrong with my behaviour. I was sick all the time – if it wasn't a headache, it was abdominal pains. When I had left home to come to university in Cape Town, I had felt relieved and thought that I would start life afresh, unaware that there are certain things in your life that cannot be forgotten. I was haunted by memories of my life back home.

I was having difficulty coping but I didn't trust Alan enough to talk to him about things. I knew he was there and that was all I wanted. When I found out about the affair, I knew what it meant: Alan was abandoning me. I knew that, though he cared about me, he was beginning to feel deprived of certain things in our relationship. He started being mean to me and we stopped going to town together. He no longer found my jokes funny. We fought about almost everything and he put me down at every opportunity. I had hurt him by telling him I was not in love with him, that I was doing him a favour by being seen with him.

I confronted him about the affair and he did not deny it. He told me that both the other girl and I were his girlfriends. I did not understand that. I asked him to leave me, lacking the courage to break off the relationship myself. At least if he left me, I would be able to blame him for my resulting unhappiness.

I went to see the other girl, who admitted to having a relationship with Alan and said she knew about me as well. Later that day she walked into Alan's room and found me in there. There was a serious confrontation and Alan slapped my face in front of his new girlfriend. His behaviour along with the ongoing affair made me very upset. He had not only humiliated me and was about to abandon me, he had now invaded my body with the slap. He deserved to die and pay for his sins and those of others. I could not understand why the lady at the Student Counselling Centre thought it was more than that.

'Do you really think your boyfriend deserved to be killed just for that?' asked the counsellor.

'Yes,' I replied.

The counsellor knew I was not cooperating and so she asked me to write down a story about my family back home – how I had grown up and the things that had happened to me. We were going to look at it and talk about it at our next session.

I made sure I did not return for any other sessions. I was not ready to talk about why I had wanted to kill Alan. He was paying for something I had held onto for a long time. It was not my fault. It wasn't until I got myself equipped to deal with the realities of my childhood that I could put definitions to my feelings and events. I came from a culture of silence, a culture of a lack of knowledge and a culture of 'It is not just you, everyone else has the same problems, so get over it!'

Two years later I graduated from university with an Honours degree and went to work in Johannesburg. I had finally broken up with Alan after we had both tried several times to make the relationship work. Things had gone from bad to worse since the fight. We tried to work it out but I found myself so attracted to other men that I always left Alan to be with someone else. Even those other men could not get me to stay. I was determined to break their hearts. I could not, indeed did not want to, hold on to a man. I often ran before I got hurt or abandoned. I wanted to protect myself, even if it meant hurting others in the process. I was unable to forgive Alan for what he had done to me and our fight was always hanging over our relationship. Finally I decided to move on for good.

8

'How many cigarettes does your father smoke in a day? One, two, three . . .' This was one of the games my friends and I used to play when we were young. The number you chose would be used to count round the girls and the one on whom it ended was required to say how many cigarettes her father smoked. It was the only time I had to say something about my father in front of other kids. My father never smoked but in the game that did not matter. Most of the children I played with had fathers and while some of them were not working at all, others had jobs in Johannesburg. At least my friends knew where their fathers were and that they would see them in the December holidays. I had woken up one day to find my father gone. Although I knew he worked in Johannesburg and he only came home occasionally, this time something about his leaving was different. I had no idea when or if he would come back. I didn't ask anyone because I was never taught to ask questions, especially on matters that were termed 'adults' issues'.

I had never had any way of communicating with my father while he was at work, so although I felt there was something strange about his leaving, I could not contact him to find out if he was coming back or not. I had to continue living without any explanation as to what had happened to him. Since we had moved from my father's village, I had seen less of him but like any little girl I waited and waited for him to come back.

One day, after a long time had passed, I overheard my mother saying on the phone that she was going to get a divorce from my father. At the time, the word 'divorce' was unknown to me and I could not understand why my mother would use the strange word when talking about my father. He had been gone for a long time by then and it was obvious he was not coming back, but why my mother should use the word 'divorce' about him was a mystery to me. Due to my insecurities, I had a tendency to watch my mother's every move. I was forever trying to make sense of the woman I had come to fear and from whom I was totally detached. I blamed her for my sufferings and in my childish state of awareness, I noted everything in silence.

The conversation my mother was having was becoming intense. 'I *am* going to get a divorce. My lawyers are working on it. He is not coming back here again. I am sick of his irresponsibility. We are going to court to finalise the matter.'

'Divorce', 'lawyers', 'irresponsibility', 'court', I thought to myself. These were big words and I was having trouble understanding them. I knew that Mr Rabothata was a lawyer but I didn't know much about what lawyers actually did. He had helped the family when Angela had her car accident, and he was an uncle to our family friends, so I knew him very well. As for the words 'divorce', 'irresponsibility' and 'court', I had not heard them before. No one in our community discussed things like that. Most fathers just disappeared like mine had. I knew that those men were *mafamolele*, meaning men who went to work and never came back home. My one uncle was one of them, as was our neighbour. Those men left their wives and children all alone.

Now it was happening in my own home but our situation was different because it had many strange words attached to it instead of the usual explanation of *mafamolele*. As I eavesdropped on my mother's conversation, I decided she was being cruel. I started blaming her for my father's disappearance. I believed she had made my father leave and now she was doing the 'divorce thing' on him. I was not allowed to ask any questions because I was too young and it would have been disrespectful for me to interfere in adults' matters. But I started keeping an eye on my mother in an effort to hear more about the 'divorce'. I wanted to know what else she was saying about my father. I never spoke to my brothers and sister about the conversation, nor did I discuss it with my friends, and my mother told me nothing.

Days, months, years went by and I still hoped that my father would return. I didn't hear from him or see him in all that time. I was angry but I did not tell anyone. Most terribly, I blamed my mother for every mishap in my life and our family. I wanted to defend my father but I did not know why or from what I should defend him. I felt betrayed and lonely. My waiting continued and my mother's unavailability due to her work pressures made things worse. I now believed that both my mother and father had betrayed and abandoned me. I also strongly believed that my mother had not liked my father very much. On the few occasions they had been together, I remembered my parents being cold towards each other. They were not excited around each other and I had thought it was an adult thing. I could not discuss my fears and anger with my siblings. We were taught never to talk about such matters.

One day my mother was very angry with Sipho and I heard her say something I did not like: 'You are untidy, irresponsible and naive – just like your father.'

Those words made me feel even more anger towards her but she didn't notice. Our relationship was such that we never had any lengthy conversations and so she was not aware of my anguish and hatred towards her. The words my mother spoke to Sipho told me that she thought of my father as a filthy, useless person because Sipho at that moment was looking dirty and was acting very irresponsibly. He was coming home very late, he would talk back to her and he was becoming a bully.

I closed my ears to anything nice my mother might say about my father. Not that there were many discussions about him anyway – it was just an occasional remark here and there. I also never wanted to share anything with my mother because I would be thought of as trying to cause trouble. Most of my silence was self-imposed out of fear of not being heard and confusion around the events in my home and in the village. My aunt who worked in Johannesburg had contact with my father. One day she mentioned she had come across him in Johannesburg. I watched my mother's reaction to the news. Her nonchalant response confirmed for me that she really did not like him any more. It was obvious to me that my mother knew where my father was but she could not be bothered to go and look for him or see him.

Each time I looked at photographs of my father, I saw myself. Relatives also remarked on how much I looked like him – a very dark, handsome man with beautifully crafted features. I did not know what had happened between my parents that made my father never come back. It would have been disrespectful for me to question my mother about it.

As more and more time passed, I stopped waiting for my father to come back. Instead, I watched to see if my mother was going to replace him. My view was that she was not allowed to have a man in her life any more.

Eleven years later, on my way to the airport and on to university life in Cape Town, I saw my father again for the first time. This happened because Sipho had disappeared from home and my mother discovered that he had gone to visit our father. She thought we should go and fetch Sipho on our way to the airport, and she told me it would be my opportunity to tell my father that I was now going to university. By this time, I had completely detached myself from my father. I felt no emotions regarding his disappearance any more. I had buried them in my subconscious. More than anything, I had enough of my own problems to occupy my confused world. I could not see where my father might fit into my life any more. I had channelled all my anger and experiences through to other areas of my life, such as watching my mother and wanting to leave home so badly, that I did not know how to respond to the news of seeing him again.

When we arrived in Johannesburg, we went to Alexandra to my mother's uncle who was going to take us to my father's place. When we got there, my father was alone in a dark, empty house that had no signs of happiness or life in it.

'Hello,' was all I said to him.

'How are you, my child? I have heard you are now going to the university. I am very proud of you, my girl,' he said, looking at me in the candlelight.

The house had no electricity and I was shocked at the bad condition it was in. I could see his huge eyes looking at me with love and sadness. Sadness, perhaps, because I no longer knew him. I could not even be happy to see him; I had no feelings about the meeting at all. I simply stood there saying nothing. I was confused myself.

'Where is Sipho? Is he here with you? We have come to fetch him. He must say goodbye to his sister and he also needs to come back home and go to school,' my mother said after a long moment of silence.

'Yes, he is here. But he has gone out for the moment. He arrived two weeks ago. I was going to send him home but I had no money. I told him to wait until I got paid so that I could give him the bus fare,' replied my father.

There was lot of tension in the dark house. I was grateful for the poor lighting so that I did not have to read the expressions in my parents' eyes – and they could not read mine. Sipho walked in and our mother was not happy to see him at all. She started

page
87

shouting about how irresponsible he was and how his father was corrupting him.

'We are leaving now; I want you back home tomorrow. I am on my way to the airport taking your sister. I do not want to come looking for you again,' my mother said angrily.

Sipho did not answer. He just looked at our mother and sat down next to our father. I also stood there silently watching my father's reaction towards my mother. Although he was angry, he tried to be calm. He did not want to talk too much. He promised my mother that Sipho would be sent back home. Then he told me to have a nice trip to Cape Town and that he would have given me some pocket money but he was broke. We said our goodbyes and left the house. My father had aged and he looked very tired and unhappy. He had also mentioned that he was not feeling well. I had waited for so many years for him to come back into my life and now I struggled to connect with him. I had always blamed my mother for my father leaving but now when I looked at him I saw an irresponsible person who I was not proud to call my father any more. I had managed for so long without him that he no longer felt like an important part of my life.

When I next saw my father, it was five years later at my graduation party. My mother had told me she thought it was important to invite him to the party. I did not have much to say on the subject. I was so excited about graduating that nothing else mattered much. On the day, I greeted him and that was as far as our interaction went. While at university I had worked to erase all memories of my father from my mind. I never spoke about him with my friends and had even told them that he had died a long time ago. The more I said it, the more real it became for me.

A year after my graduation party, I received a phone call from my mother informing me that my father was at home in poor health. She asked me to come and see him because she did not think he was going to live for very long. As usual, I did not ask her many questions. I made a plan to go home over the weekend and then I received a message on my phone.

'This is your mother; please call me as soon as possible. Your father passed away this morning.'

I did not know what to do. In bewilderment, I threw away the phone and screamed. However, the minute my tears came rolling down, I blocked them. My friend and flat-mate Bontle was with me and asked what was wrong. I told her about the message and I grew even more confused as I said the words. Over the years I had managed to kill my father so that I did not have to wait for him any more. Now he had died in reality and I did not know how to express my feelings appropriately. I eventually allowed my tears to flow when Bontle hugged me – the first and only time I cried openly about my father.

I went home for the funeral and we all went to choose his coffin and make the preparations. Sipho was the one most affected by my father's passing. He cried terribly. Our other siblings seemed neutral. I did not know why they were feeling that way but I also did not show any emotions.

All our relatives arrived to bury my father. People I had never met before were introduced to me for the first time as my father's siblings and relatives. At last I began to have an understanding of who my father was. I made many interesting discoveries during the funeral, discoveries that were helpful, confusing and upsetting all at the same time. I learned that my father had other children from another wife who had subsequently died. I had two more siblings, two half-sisters, as well as cousins from my father's brothers and sisters. Apparently I had been told about these siblings but because I was so young when it all happened and because they did not stay with us before we relocated back to my mother's village, I could not remember anything about them.

The details of my parents' relationship and marriage did not bother me because these things were part of African culture and were practised freely and openly by many people. Indeed, those 'extended' families sometimes had more stability and unity because the children had another mother to look after them even after their own mother had passed away. It was unfortunate for me that I had had no experience of meeting my half-sisters and cousins.

I also discovered that after he had retired, my father had practised as an *inyanga* (a traditional doctor) in Johannesburg. And he had been staying with another woman after he left us. I was disappointed that he was not the model father that I had imagined and defended in my mind all the time.

Towards the end of his life, when he was alone and sick, there was no one to look after him. He had remained in contact with his other children so they knew where he was and went to fetch him. When they could no longer afford to care for him, they brought him back to my mother. Despite the fact that they were divorced she did her duty until he died.

While I was trying to put together the pieces of the puzzle that was my father, I wondered why his marriage to my mother had not lasted. I asked my mother some questions but I knew I had limitations as to what I could ask.

At first all I could think about was how much I had not known about him and how much I would have loved to get to know him. But then I had to make a decision; I decided that I could not allow other people to tell me who my father was because they might have their own pre-conceived ideas about him and all the beautiful memories I had of him would be destroyed. I had to be satisfied with the little time I had spent with him and with the little information I already knew about him. I wondered what it was my father had shared with Sipho that made my brother so sad at his funeral. I also wondered what all his other children had shared with him. I could not know all of the answers to my questions and so I simply tried to make peace with the fact that I was his daughter. Some things about my father would always remain a mystery to me.

9

Now my father was dead for real. I thought I had killed him in my mind a long time ago and that his actual death could not make any material difference in my life. Of course, I had not really killed him at all; I had simply blocked out everything about him. Unconsciously I was still looking for him and I unknowingly began a mission to replace him. I thought that if I found a man I could hold on to, my life would be better. I hoped that if I could be a good girl, the man would love me and I would forget all about my pain. I wanted to find someone who could rescue me, and I was determined that this time around I would try to sustain the relationship.

With Timothy, things started very slowly. When I met him, he had been recently divorced and had just ended a relationship with his live-in girlfriend. The divorce papers were not yet final but I told myself I was not part of the problem that had broken the marriage so I had nothing to worry about. Later I found out that he had broken it off with his girlfriend as soon as he met me.

He was a most charming person and I thought he could offer me the kind of rescue I needed. I reasoned that if I helped him to sort out his life and became the centre of his attention, he would love me and adore me forever. That is what a little girl does with her father – she makes him her hero and she becomes the apple of his eye. The more I gave into the idea, the more I found myself on an emotional see-saw. One month Tim's mood was good and I was content and the next month, out of nowhere, I was no longer needed in his life. I held on to the hope that things would get better but the more I stayed, the more unstable and insecure the situation became.

I didn't even have to make Tim angry, or fight with him; he had a way of making sure he put me in the wrong and let me blame myself for it. It was as if he knew he was dealing with a wounded person. We could be arguing about my missing an appointment we had by ten minutes and I would be told 'this relationship is over'. Then he would disappear, only to show up two weeks later pretending nothing had changed.

I was dumped more than fifteen times in the course of our relationship and on each occasion I felt guilty because he would not tell me why he acted as he did. The more I gave into the instability of the relationship, the more I lost my self-esteem. My true self was buried even deeper.

'I think you should see Dr Gijima; she is good with counselling when it comes to relationship issues.' This was my friend, Girly, who thought I needed to talk to someone after she heard that Tim had dumped me yet again.

Dr Gijima wanted to know why I stayed in such a dysfunctional relationship. 'Tell me about your previous relationships. How did they end?' she asked.

'I ended all of them,' I replied. 'The one that lasted the longest was Alan. Four years ago, while still at university, we had a major fight that I blamed Alan for. The events that led to the fight and the fight itself made it difficult for me to want to repair the relationship even though we tried for three more years to make it work. I kept having flashbacks to what happened on that day. Our intimacy in the relationship died completely. I could not allow him to touch me any more. I still wonder why he put up with my rejection for such a long time. If he did touch me, I would lie there motionless, wanting him to leave me alone. I remember that one day he even told me he thought I was still mad at him for having cheated on me while at university.'

I was still not ready to talk about why I had wanted to kill Alan. I thought that the reason I had come to see Dr Gijima was to fix my relationship with Tim. I was beginning to think I was unable to keep a man.

'I wonder why you would carry that thing with you for so long?' Alan asked me sadly. 'I thought it was part of our past. How can you hold a grudge for such a long time? I care about you and it hurts me that you reject me like this. I will hold on until you are able to forgive me one day.'

When Alan said this it had been six months since we had made love. He loved me but I was unable to reciprocate his feelings.

It was undeniable that I wanted to be loved. I was eager to find love and hold on to it and my eagerness turned into desperation and anxiety. I had no idea how to find that love, let alone interact with men on an intimate emotional level. I could not admit that I had never had a positive male role model in my life. I had always been surrounded by many women: my mother, grandmother, sister, aunts, cousins and female teachers. I learned certain behaviours through them and through the culture of secrecy and silence we lived in. If something was not told to me loud and clear, I would either find out about it from my peers or silently draw my own conclusions.

Now I was experiencing the natural instinct of wanting to have a relationship, get married and have children. These things would have meant as much to me, if not more, than my academic and material success. I had landed a job in Johannesburg with a multinational conglomerate, was renting a townhouse in a luxurious urban suburb, was driving my own car and was counted amongst the successful girls from my village and community. But I yearned for love.

Tim had been my boyfriend for only seven months and I was already feeling abandoned and unhappy. This time around I had gone to see Dr Gijima because I was determined to fix the relationship; I wanted to make Tim stay. He had first broken up with me just three months after we started dating. He blamed our cultural differences and said that his parents would disown him if he continued to date a woman from a different ethnic group. I begged him to give me a chance to prove that people did not have to come from the same ethnic group to have a successful relationship. I went from being happy about my new-found love to being insecure and confused.

Two weeks later, he returned and told me to forget what he said about his parents' disapproval of me because he would not allow them to rule his affairs. I was ecstatic. Then he broke it off again four months later over an argument about me not getting to an appointment on time. That was when I started to doubt myself and went to see Dr Gijima to find out exactly what was wrong with me. Why couldn't I make him happy? He would go from being so much in love and wanting to be with me forever, to feeling absolutely nothing for me. His behaviour, approach to problems and lack of commitment showed his lack of desire to have a meaningful relationship with me. But to me his behaviour suggested that I was unworthy of having a healthy relationship and of being loved.

'Tell me more about the fight with Alan. How did it start and what happened?' asked Dr Gijima.

'He had hurt me and I wanted to kill him.'

There was a pause and I started to cry. I was going to have to tell now. I had never told anyone before. On the evening after the fight I wrote in my journal that I was angry with Alan because he

94

had reminded me of the first man who had hurt me when I was just six years old. I wanted him to pay.

Dr Gijima asked me to bring the journal to our next session the following week. Together we read it. The stories in my journal showed that I had a long way to go. The therapy sessions now turned to the core of my problems; I had many things to unravel.

I wanted to hold on to Tim and our relationship and so I ignored the signs which showed that Tim had issues of his own. The fact that he was very secretive and mysterious drew me to him. At least I did not have to focus on myself. I felt I had a responsibility towards him and our relationship. The search to figure out who this mysterious person really was shifted the focus from my own issues. I got more and more hooked into his life, and all the uncertainty that came with the emotional blackmail to which he subjected me did not matter. All I wanted was someone who could make me forget about my past. I thought I was in love. I could not see all the early signs of an unhealthy relationship and that the way in which Tim treated me was unacceptable. No matter how much Dr Gijima told me it was not my fault and that I needed to take control of who I was in the relationship and what it was that I wanted and what was acceptable to me, I did not know how to break free.

I often felt I had to be on my guard in case I made him angry, for when that happened he would not talk to me for a week. My brain knew there was nothing in the relationship but my heart wanted me to stay so that I could start a family for myself.

Timothy was seeing other women and I often knew about them but his attitude was 'I don't owe you anything'. One day when I found him in the house with another woman, he told me: 'I don't love you, I never did and I never will. So I have a right to do what I want with my life.'

Even after this incident, I still took him back when he came begging me to give us another chance. I began to feel as if he was doing me a favour each time he asked me to take him back after he went off for two weeks. I would sit crying for hours over my lack of ability to keep a man.

Dr Gijima constantly told me it was not my fault he behaved this way and that I had a choice to walk away from the relationship while I could still save my soul. I did try to break it off twice myself but failed both times. Tim simply told me he was not going anywhere because he knew I loved him. 'It is going to be difficult for you to get rid of me,' he told me.

Each time I thought of leaving Tim, I thought of myself as a failure, a failure because I could not keep my relationship going. I had to do it. No one in my family was married; those who did tie the knot never stayed that way for long and I was determined to break the pattern. I took comfort in knowing that at least Tim still wanted to be with me even if he felt no love at all. It was a silent deal we had made: he was doing me a favour and I was willing to surrender myself in return for the favour.

During our relationship, my abdominal pains became increasingly severe. I was unable to enjoy our sexual encounters and Tim couldn't understand my lack of sexual appetite. We fought a lot about it. He told me he did not feel loved any more.

Over the years I had been to many different doctors in an attempt to sort out my ongoing abdominal pains but they were never able to get to the root of my problems. Some doctors thought I had Pelvic Inflammatory Disease and tests were also run for various sexually transmitted diseases. One doctor even told me he thought I had chronic abdominal pain, and when they could not find anything, I lived on antibiotics and pills to stop the bleeding. By this time, my menstrual pains had evolved into very severe abdominal and lower back pains that radiated down my legs. If I was not suffering from extremely heavy menstrual flow accompanied by a lot of clotting, I would bleed moderately for more than two weeks. I also experienced abdominal bloating. The pain was almost constant – before, during and after my periods, and during and after intercourse. When I lost interest in lovemaking I got very worried as I thought I was to be denied its pleasures.

Now that I was working, the pain started interfering with my life and I was forced to stay away from work on a regular basis. But I refused to go to any more doctors because I was tired of not finding a cure, or at least a reason for what I was going through.

I started dealing with the pain by lying naked on the floor in the kitchen so that the discomfort of the cold floor took my mind off the pain. I would scream for God to come and take me because I could not take the pain any more.

I was anxious about the pain's interference and its ability to destroy the relationship I was determined to build and sustain, and so I begged Dr Gijima to help me. I linked the pain and the heavy and irregular bleeding to the abortion I had had and also thought that it might relate to having had my virginity broken at age six. I knew that I had had lots of vaginal fluids and discharge from an early age though I did not have a definition for what they were.

Above all, my main worry was that I was being punished for having killed my baby. I was concerned I would not be able to have other children if the pain persisted. Perhaps it was even a sign, as my mother had told me, *o na le noga ye mpe*, meaning 'you have a bad womb'. According to my cultural beliefs, a woman who suffered from severe pains and prolonged bleeding was barren. I believed that this would cause problems for me when I wanted to have children. I would need to find someone to *kgaola noga ya ka*, meaning that my prolonged periods would be cut off using traditional African *muti* (medicine) mixtures and certain rituals would be performed to make sure I conceived.

I must have angered both God and my ancestors, I thought. I should have died from the abortion. I remembered that while I was in pain during the abortion process, I had had flashing images of my late great-grandmother and of my cousin Pinky who had died from a backstreet abortion. To me this was an indication that I was supposed to have died, yet I survived.

I discussed my feelings about the abortion with Dr Gijima and we worked to separate the issues involved – the psychological and physical after-effects of my abortion and my fear of not being able to have any more children. I told Dr Gijima that I felt God must be punishing me for having had the abortion.

When we were exploring the various psychological effects of my abortion, I spoke about all the fears that I had about the abortion itself. I wanted to know if I could be forgiven for the abortion, how the fetus must have felt about me and whether I was being punished for having killed him. The sight of red meat disgusted and repulsed me. I was terrified of the smell of blood. I could not look at small babies without thinking about that day. In our discussions I kept referring to the fetus as 'the thing' or 'it' and I was not comfortable with this.

'Have you ever thought of giving your aborted son a name?' Dr Gijima asked. 'That will help his memory to rest in peace and you will be able to forgive yourself if you know you are dealing with a departed human being and not an "it" or a "thing".'

My eyes welled up with tears. 'Thabo is what I would like to call him; it means Joy,' I said, covering my mouth with my hand to take a deep breath.

'That is a beautiful name, Kedibone. At least now we can honour him while you forgive yourself for not having thought of him as a departed human being but as an "it" or a "thing".'

'I sometimes wonder what he would be like. He would be six this year and I would like to at least say something to him. I don't know why but I think there is something I should say to him,' I said sadly.

'I think it would be best if you wrote Thabo a letter. What do you think? You can bring the letter with you to the next session if you want or you can keep it for yourself.'

That night when I got home I wrote:

Dear Thabo,

To honour your spirit, I named you Thabo when I first spoke about you with Dr Gijima. I can still see your tiny four-month-old body lying on the floor attached to me through the umbilical cord. I remember your heartbeat and your head the size of my fist while I screamed for the nurses to come and help me because I was afraid you were going to bite me. I watched your heart stop beating after they cut the umbilical cord and your tiny body eventually lying still on the floor. Although I was crying because of the pain, something inside me died with you. The horror of having to wait while you were fighting for your life inside me after the abortion took a part of me along with your soul. The memories and the images of your body have haunted me for a long time – when I have to eat meat, when I go to sleep and every time I see a small baby. I did not think you would allow me the opportunity to mother another child.

My son, I want you to forgive me for I have struggled for so long to forgive myself. I will always cherish the memories of your life growing inside of me. I will remember you for the short time that we shared the same food and breathed the same air. I pray that God will send me other children and I will carry the strength your terrible death gave me for life.

May your soul rest in peace.

Love, Mommy

I felt very relieved after I had written the letter and wished that someone had suggested it to me before. I now felt able to acknowledge the psychological impact that the abortion had had on my life and my feelings around the whole incident. I was still desperate to understand why I was struggling physically with so many vaginal infections and so much pain. I did not think I had any sexually transmitted diseases because I always insisted that Tim and I use a condom. I knew about the dangers of HIV/Aids and was determined to avoid them. Were my physical problems a result of the abortion or not?

Even as I took a decision to do all I could to improve my relationship with Tim, things became worse. I had felt something like a ball moving inside my womb, and then later, the ball seemed to diminish in size while I was bleeding heavily with smelly clotting. Several months later, I missed my periods and then I started feeling the ball moving again in my tummy. Three days later, very dark clots with a foul smell started coming out. I thought I must have been pregnant and now I was miscarrying. A friend referred me to her gynaecologist. It appeared that the bleeding was caused by the breakdown of a sizeable cyst in one of my ovaries. I suffered lower back pain and cramps for the whole week while the cyst broke down.

Then the doctor hospitalised me so that he could perform a laparoscopy. For the first time I learned the name of my condition – 'endometriosis'. I did not know what it meant.

My gynaecologist explained to me that endometriosis is a condition where the endometrium (the lining of the uterus) is found in locations outside the uterus. The misplaced tissue may be found on the ovaries, uterus, bowel, bladder, utero-sacral ligaments (ligaments that hold the uterus in place) or the peritoneum (lining of the pelvis and abdominal cavity).

To me, all this was medical and scientific jargon that I could not understand. The doctor also told me that the condition could start any time between a woman's first and last period. I was frightened by the idea that women with endometriosis struggle to become pregnant, and despite my therapy sessions with Dr Gijima I still felt that if I, too, struggled, it would not be because of the endometriosis but because I was being punished for the abortion.

The doctor's initial treatment was to put me on a birth control injection in order to regulate my cycle. However, the injection did not help. I started having bad side effects and gained excessive weight. I bled continuously and become anaemic and very fatigued. At this point my sexual desires deteriorated tremendously and my self-esteem was taking a knock due to the weight I was gaining. I remember the embarrassment I felt one day when someone I had not seen in a long time asked: 'When is your little one due?' Although I laughed the question off, I was very hurt. It was ironic that while I was terrified by the thought of not being able to conceive, I was walking around looking pregnant.

Along with trying to deal with my condition through my therapy sessions, I started doing some research about endometriosis. I wanted to know what caused it if it was not the abortion. Some of the theories suggested that it could be caused by abnormal functioning of the immune system, retrograde (or reflux) menstruation in which some menstrual blood flows backward through the fallopian tubes, and genetic or hereditary factors. I learned there was no cure but proper treatment was available to relieve the symptoms. I was always fighting infections and had been put on antidepressants twice. Perhaps my constant stress and depression had weakened my body's ability to fight disease and that was how the endometriosis had developed.

My roller-coaster relationship with Tim continued although I was finding his pattern of behaviour a little more bearable. His mood swings and the silent treatment were always followed by an overwhelming excitement. When the whole cycle began, I knew I should ignore him and carry on with life until he got himself into a better mood. For the whole week I knew I should not talk, ask questions, get in his way, or call him at work to find out about his day or ask him why he was working late. I felt I was managing the situation.

Unfortunately, while dealing with my pain, I also had to handle the realities of my work situation. I was no longer productive and found no fulfilment in the job any more. I realised I was only there to make a living and to make sure I continued proving to my community back home that I was successful. It was not a surprise to me when I lost my job. I had seen it coming.

I was called into my manager's office a week after I came back from a long period of sick leave. We had a chat about my health, my financial situation and my unfulfilling career. I had developed terrible sinusitis and I felt as though if I was not bleeding excessively, I was sneezing continuously.

Finally my manager said to me: 'I'm sorry, but we don't think we have a use for you any more.' Initially I thought I had lost my job because of my many absences from work. I lashed out and accused him of blackmailing me because I had shared with him that I was unhappy with my job and needed a challenge.

He replied that I should see this retrenchment as an opportunity for me to move on and find something else that I would enjoy doing. If I chose to stay I would be demoted and might not be so lucky in the next round of retrenchments that he was sure was coming. I knew very well what he meant: six months after I had been employed, a lot of the new graduate trainees I had started with were retrenched. I had been lucky then so the chances of my being lucky again were very slim.

I stormed out of my manager's office and went straight to the toilets to cry. I was desperately scared of the unknown. Despite the fact that I found my job boring and unfulfilling I could not afford to be without it. I had always considered myself fortunate because I had been recruited while busy with my final exams. I had not had to job-hunt but now I would have to go out and look for work. I was also scared about breaking the news to my family and friends.

Ntombi, a friend and colleague, followed me to the toilets to find out what was happening. All I could say was: 'How am I going to tell my mother that I do not have a job any more and what about my car and my flat? Who is going to pay for all my expenses?'

'Try not to take it so personally,' Ntombi said. 'These things do happen, you know. It is possible that more people in the organisation will be told the same thing. Did he tell you if there are others on the list?' Ntombi had always been there to comfort me. She was the first person I had spoken to about the rape incidents in my past when I was ready to talk about them during my therapy. Ntombi also knew all about the ups and downs in my relationship with Tim. She had always advised me to walk away and start afresh but now she thought that Tim would at least be able to help me through the news of losing my job.

'I think you should phone Tim and let him know.'

I did just that; I was not interested in finding out if there were more people in the organisation who were being told to leave. From the toilets, I phoned Tim to tell him the news. He assured me that we would talk about it at home that evening. Then I called Dr Gijima because I felt as though my misery was nowhere near ending. I needed to speak to someone who would give me strength to face the day. Dr Gijima suggested I come to see her the next day. She also suggested I call one of my friends or family members for support and I phoned my cousin Reneilwe who was very comforting.

When I went back to the office to pack my things, I found another woman with whom I worked in tears. Then our manager's office door opened and another colleague walked out looking very miserable. I knew why. I had been the first one to be told about the organisation's plans to downsize; now others were hearing the news. Some two hundred employees were leaving, including my manager, but I couldn't have known it when he spoke to me. The knowledge that many other people were going through the same thing did not help me feel any better.

I went straight home with no idea of what was going to happen to me next. The lease agreement for my flat was expiring at the end of the month and I knew I could not extend it without a secure income. Tim promised he would help me and said I could move in with him. I was initially very happy but that did not last long. When a month passed without me finding another job, things started to go sour between us. He was no longer pleased I was in the house. I tried so hard to hold on to the hope that things would work out, while he, by contrast, showed no signs of genuine happiness about the relationship. He was always guarded with his emotions and could sometimes go for a week and a half without talking to me. When I confronted him in an attempt to understand what was happening, he told me he no longer felt loved by me. He also said he could not afford to have me in the house if I was not helping with the rent and household expenses.

Although I had been given a severance package, I thought Tim had agreed that the money was to be used in case it took me a while to find another job. I had also just damaged my car in a terrible accident and needed money to pay for the insurance excess. The arrangement I had with Tim was that I would stay and look for a job while we worked on strengthening our relationship. He had told me not to worry about anything because he believed in me and he knew I would get another job soon. I mistakenly interpreted this as a sign of love and contentment in the relationship. He went into a pattern of mood swings, coming back very late from work, never wanting to be seen in public with me, and complaining about me, constantly criticising my qualities and everything I did.

When I protested, I received an email asking me to leave as I was disturbing the peace in the house. His short message shocked me and I phoned Ntombi to come and read the email with me.

I had to be honest with her with regard to the situation at Tim's house since I had moved in. Ntombi knew how determined I was to make the relationship work and she suggested that I phone my therapist.

Dr Gijima advised me to move out immediately without trying to argue or attempting to fix things any further.

She told me, 'At the moment, Kedibone, you are in no state to deal with the stress this situation with Tim is going to bring. You need to give him and yourself some space while you deal with your retrenchment.'

Ntombi supported Dr Gijima's advice. Before Tim got home, I packed my things and left, moving in with my friend Gertrude. I continued to feel sorry for myself and guilty that somehow I kept making Tim angry. Tim never bothered to look for me or find out how I was.

Now I had no job, no car, no boyfriend and no flat to call my own. At least my car was being fixed at the panel beaters. Unfortunately, Gertrude had to move to a different city, which meant I had to find an alternative place to live. I stayed with another friend for two weeks but left when she suddenly demanded rent when we had agreed that I could stay there for free. I was now going through job interviews that not only drained me, they also reminded me that the world can be a cruel place. Since I had no transport, I was unable to attend my therapy sessions, though I did talk on the telephone with Dr Gijima.

I moved in with my cousin Moyahabo who was renting a room in a house and finally got my car back after six weeks of waiting. One day when I came back from the gym, I walked in on some church people holding a service in the house. I was asked to come to the front and was told to raise my hands and pray to God to forgive me for not having attended the service.

When I refused, I was told to pray to God to forgive me for being stubborn and to tell God that for as long as I stayed in the house with my cousin, I would pray and worship with them. The owner of the house said I should tell God that I was insecure and my insecurity had made me a stubborn and disobedient person. Shocked, I walked out. Maybe I was insecure, but I did not need a stranger to embarrass me in front of a room full of people. I felt even more sorry for myself.

A few hours later I received a call from Moyahabo, telling me that the owner of the house had said that I should not return unless I apologised for embarrassing her. I left and now had to find another place. I moved to my friend Nthabiseng but could not stay there for long because she was living with her boyfriend. Nothing was forthcoming on the job front and I was deeply miserable as I contemplated my remaining few options. Should I go back home to my mother's house and face the difficulties of looking for a job there? I had by now gathered the strength to tell my mother about my recent job loss. She was very worried and encouraged me to keep the faith and never cease to pray. I even thought about killing myself but I didn't want to die.

Then I remembered that my cousin Reneilwe owned a house, though she lived about forty-five minutes away from the city. I spoke to her and she agreed to accommodate me and my furniture, which had been in storage while I had been moving from one place to another. At least there was room for the two of us and I did not mind driving to the city.

I went to stay with Reneilwe but on the second day there, I was so depressed that I needed to run away from everyone and the pain I was feeling. After Reneilwe had left for work, I got into the car with my clothes and just drove away. I didn't know where I was going but the idea of being stranded on the road seemed much better than facing my sorrows there. I cried as I drove, finally ending up in Bloemfontein. I put in petrol and phoned a friend I knew there who was able to provide a bed for me that night.

I did not tell my friend why I was travelling; I said I was on holiday. The following morning I left to continue my journey. Reneilwe was very worried. She had looked everywhere for me. Although I kept my phone on, I was not taking any calls from her. I also ignored all her text messages. She was pleading with me at least to tell her where I was and why I had left without saying anything.

One message read: 'I am aware there is nothing I can do to fix your problems. I cannot give you your life back. I cannot repair your relationship with Tim. But I am your sister and I love you very much. Your pain is my pain.'

I cried when I read that because, while I knew Reneilwe cared, seeing the words brought it home. But I still did not take her calls or respond to her messages. Reneilwe realised my mother would panic if she knew what was happening with her daughter. Instead, she phoned Gertrude, Moyahabo, and even Alan. Reneilwe had known Alan while he and I were still dating. She knew she would not get anything out of Tim since he had not bothered to find out where I was after I moved out of his house.

Alan phoned me pretending at first not to know what was happening. The two of us had managed to put our differences aside and we had become good friends. Alan knew I was seeing Dr Gijima. Although he had no details as to why I was seeing her, he was sure that whatever we were working through was in my best interests. He had seen me in the worst of situations; visiting me three years previously when I was admitted for the first time to a psychiatric hospital for stress and depression. He still cared a lot about me. Later in our conversation he told me that I should go back home to Reneilwe.

'Do you how much pain you are causing your cousin? She phoned me in tears. Gertrude also phoned begging me to talk to you. Please tell me where you are. If you are too far to drive back, I will come and fetch you myself,' he offered.

His brother, who was very fond of me, also came to the phone to try to convince me to come back home. I still refused to tell them anything, even pretending that I had not left town and expressing surprise that Reneilwe would tell them such a lie. Then I hung up on them.

After ignoring everyone's pleas for me to come home, I decided to drive to Cape Town. Though I had started having panic attacks, I was determined to go as far away as possible from my pain and fears. Suddenly the car stopped and I could not start it again. I got out and asked for help from passing cars. Some men helped me get to a safe place. I called Dr Gijima and told her that I was scared.

'Why don't you come to my office for a session? I will see you as soon as you arrive. I know we have not been having our sessions since have not had your car. I also understand that since you are unemployed you could be thinking of how you will pay me. I am not going to be billing you at all. I want you to come see me.'

Dr Gijima did not tell me she was already aware of what was happening. I learned later that Alan and my cousins had contacted her for help.

I had to explain that I was six hours' drive away from her office. I told her all that had happened and how I had ignored my friends' calls. I was now frightened because my car had stopped.

'Then why don't you phone your cousin Reneilwe to come and fetch you?' Dr Gijima suggested. 'She must be very worried about you.'

I made the call and Reneilwe sent some friends from Bloem-fontein to fetch me. A garage repaired my car and I drove back to stay with her again. Though we never spoke about the details of the incident, we agreed that our parents back home should not know about it.

I resumed my therapy sessions with Dr Gijima. I already had a problem with my identity because of my past, now losing my job meant another real crisis of confidence. Since my retrenchment three months before I had gradually stopped believing I had any potential to make it in life. To me, my job and the organisation I worked for represented an achievement, an indication of success and progress. When I had joined the company, all of my peers had envied me because it was an international organisation that every graduate dreamed of working for.

Now, during my job-hunting excursions, I became impatient with the recruiters. At one interview I told a woman she could keep her job after being asked to write a series of aptitude tests. I felt humiliated because I had never taken tests like those in my life before. I found some of the questions that people asked me very embarrassing and demeaning. When I was asked: 'Do you consider yourself a very stable person?' I couldn't frame a proper answer.

After struggling for months with job interviews and ongoing uncertainty, I was employed by another organisation where I told myself I was going to prove my potential. That was where I met my mentor and friend, Peter Kennedy, who believed in me and allowed me to empower myself. I was given an opportunity to discover what I was good at and I came to be grateful for the loss of my previous job because of the chance I was now given. I found my own place to stay back in the city and I was happy things were finally taking off.

10

If you listen to love songs such as Whitney Houston's 'Where do broken hearts go', you realise that in songs like this one, people cry over a broken relationship and beg their lost love to come back because life without them is difficult.

'Where do broken hearts go? Can they find their way home, back to the open arms, for the love that's waiting there? And if somebody loves you, won't they always love you? I look in your eyes and I know that you still care for me.'

Tim and the naive, ever-hopeful me danced to this song on the first evening he came to see me since I had moved out of his house. As I danced, I thought of how sad it is that when someone on whom you have relied decides to end a relationship, he or she takes away a piece of your heart. Even in a loveless relationship, when one partner leaves something integral is taken away, especially if there is nothing else to compare the relationship to. If you grew up without a father, it would be difficult for you to understand what it meant to be loved by a man and how you should be treated.

Tim had tracked me down and he was asking me to give our relationship another chance. Though I was reluctant, I told him I would think about it. I discussed it with Dr Gijima, who told me it was my decision to make. Ntombi made it clear to me that if I took Tim back, she would never speak to me again. My cousins told me not even to think about it. Only Gertrude thought it might work.

I was touched by Tim's willingness and determination to work harder at repairing the relationship. He wanted to start afresh and settle down. He admitted to cheating on me but assured me he had ended that relationship. He was sorry and promised to make things work, begging me to believe him. To prove his commitment he asked me to move back in with him. This was music to my ears and although I hesitated I felt honour-bound to give him another chance. It was the first time we really talked about our relationship and the things we both did to annoy each other. He told me I showed him no true love and was often distant and complained a lot. He said I did many things that reminded him of his ex-wife and his subsequent girlfriend. All they had done was nag and they had never loved him as much as he would like to be loved. This time I suggested we go for therapy because I could not understand why he kept leaving me. He agreed.

We made an appointment to see Dr Gijima together. I now shifted my focus from dealing with all the issues and problems I had started unpacking and understanding with Dr Gijima in our previous sessions. I wanted first to repair my relationship with Tim. I told myself it would form part of my progress in therapy if one thing had positive results. The rest I would sort out later. This was an opinion I held in spite of Dr Gijima's view that all my problems and behaviour were part of a pattern caused by my childhood experiences, and until I was able to deal with them and put them behind me, I was going to repeat my patterns.

The stubborn and excited me insisted we should concentrate on the relationship first. We attended our first session where we went in individually to talk about our hopes and intentions for the relationship. But when we were supposed to start with joint sessions, Tim convinced me we did not need therapy any more.

'We are doing fine. Let's postpone the therapy for now until we have finished with your move to my house. I think that we are showing progress and our determination to work on the relationship is a sign of that, don't you think?' Tim asked me.

'Well, I think you are right but we should go back as soon as we are settled in your house. We need to get to the bottom of why we experienced so many problems before. In fact, I think you should use the therapy sessions to focus on why you cheated on me.' I wanted so badly to have things straightened up. My main concern was all the women Tim had seen while we were together. I was not bothered by his attitude towards me and my own behaviour that made me stay on the roller-coaster ride of our relationship. I had decided to ignore everyone's concerns and went ahead with the move to Tim's house. I cancelled the offer-to-purchase agreement I had recently signed for my new place, moved in with Tim and seized my opportunity to work on showing him how I could truly love him.

Although I did not know it at the time, our cohabitation arrangement meant different things for us. For me, everything about the relationship was founded on the overwhelming need to be involved with somebody. I was so in need of being loved and cared for, so desperate for the security of having somebody, that I literally accepted anything.

A friend of mine told me that for some men cohabitation is part of their 'exit strategy'. They know it is easier to walk away because they often do not promise anything so they don't feel they owe anything to their partner. They play it on a trial-and-error basis, while the women concerned could easily see it as an indication of some sort of commitment.

Timothy was in our relationship for the convenience. It was cheaper for him if we went ahead and lived together. He insisted we split the expenses and that I take on the responsibility to cook, clean the house and make sure the laundry was done – something I agreed to because I thought we were both capable of paying for our expenses. We were in heaven. I was treated like a queen, showered with compliments and gifts and constantly told by Tim how much he loved me, and I was happy again. I cooked delicious meals for us, we went on vacations together and life was blissful. There was no need for us to go back to therapy at all.

I was convinced we would manage this time. We made plans to buy a bigger house and new furniture. The house we lived in was renovated and it looked beautiful and homely. I had succeeded in repairing the relationship when so many people had had no faith in it.

Ntombi was one friend I should have listened to. I had stopped talking to her because I thought she was jealous of my relationship and I was not going to allow her negativity to spoil things for me. In my renewed closeness with Tim, I even told him about Ntombi's jealousy towards us. We were bonding and strengthening our relationship by eliminating those who did not support our goal – my cousin Moyahabo and Alan included. I thought they did not have my best interests at heart.

Then came the day when I realised I was not managing the situation at all. Tim thought I had gone to visit my mother and he even phoned me to confirm it. I told him I would be away for the whole weekend but it turned out I had left it too late to leave town and instead simply went to visit an aunt.

When I returned home that evening, I discovered that my things had been removed from the bathroom and all the pictures of Tim and I had been hidden in the wardrobe. I asked him what was going on and he replied he was cleaning the house since he had thought I would be away for the weekend. He walked out while I was still talking to him and went into the lounge to watch television.

After he had left the room, his cellphone rang and I answered it. There was a woman's voice at the end of the line.

'Where are you?' she asked. 'I am here.'

Tim walked back into the room while I was still digesting what I had heard. He took the phone from me and switched it off. Then he told me I was forgiven for the crime I had committed and left the house.

I guessed that the woman had been at the gate because we had no intercom system and it was impossible to reach the house without telephoning first. She had probably reached the gate and hooted for a while before phoning.

I did not know if his behaviour was a result of general male weakness or pure infidelity on his part. Was he simply unstable or was it because I really was not good enough for him? He had me at home but he still saw himself as a single and free man who could do as he pleased, who was entitled to date other women. I would never have believed that he would go to the extent of bringing a woman into the house and sleeping with her on the very same bed that I had bought with my money, on the linen that I kept clean and looking nice.

The following day he came home all loving and apologetic, which I saw as his way of telling me how much I meant to him in spite of his behaviour.

He told me he had just been too excited and when I had told him I would be gone for the whole weekend he invited his female colleague to come and see the house. I forgave him but it was clear that we did not love each other and were in the relationship for different reasons.

Five months after the first laparoscopy I noticed the pain in my ovarian regions more frequently, coming intermittently throughout the month. Somehow I managed to soldier on until the next year, when I became very sick again. I felt that small ball once more in my tummy and the smelly clots came afterwards. The pain went from a throbbing-sharp pressure sensation to stabbing pains that made me so weak I could not walk. I stayed away from work again and this time I did not care what happened to me. Now that I was managing to build a stable relationship for myself, I told myself, I would handle the recurrence properly this time with the help of my man.

Another friend referred me to a specialist doctor who, she said, was very good with endometriosis. Although I was afraid to hope for anything, my friend told me that once the doctor had treated me, I would fall pregnant, though I did not feel ready to be pregnant. I had already talked about my fears of not having children with Dr Gijima during my therapy sessions. Now my panic attacks while driving on the freeway were getting worse and I was contemplating going back to see Dr Gijima so that she could help me deal with them. But first I had to focus on the recurrence of my endometriosis.

One doctor had told me there was a high probability I would be unable to conceive and it would be best for me to concentrate on relieving the symptoms of endometriosis and forget about having babies.

Tim told me we would be together throughout my treatment. We read about the condition from the articles and information I had collected. All of this happened in August after I had gone through another recurrence of endometriosis. In July, I had had another laparoscopy and he had been so supportive this time around and promised we would get through it together. So, I told myself, he must be genuine because he had been with me throughout the crisis. He really did not mean to have an affair. Somewhere in my heart, I knew I was lying to myself but I had not come this far to allow another woman to mess things up for us again.

The doctor said that everything was under control but if we wanted a child it was better to do it now before the condition recurred. I was supposed to wait for two months to see if my menstrual cycle was normal again and then I could decide if I wanted a baby or to be on birth control. The doctor did warn us that I could fall pregnant at any time after the procedure. But I did not think it would happen so fast and took comfort in Timothy's answer when I asked what would happen if I fell pregnant.

'It's fine, it's not like we can't have a baby and in any case we will cross that bridge when we get there. Anything to take your pain away is fine by me,' he said.

Indeed, we did have to cross the bridge – and sooner than either of us had thought.

I was excited at the possibility of having a baby, for while I always felt guilty about the abortion and endometriosis, I saw this as a chance to be forgiven for my sins. I could have a child and not feel guilty any more.

Perhaps I had misunderstood Timothy's statement and I had certainly not expected things to happen so fast. I had the surgery in July and that was the last time I saw my periods. When I went back in September for a follow-up check-up, I was told, 'Congratulations, you are six weeks pregnant!'

I was shocked and went to three other doctors to confirm my pregnancy. They all told me the same thing. Overwhelmed I went home to tell Tim the news. He jumped out of bed, furious.

'What? You mean this house is going to smell of nappies?'

That was it. I should have known then what he meant by that. He was seeing this other woman while I had unknowingly fallen pregnant already.

How could I have known if it was really love when I had never known what it felt to be truly loved and respected? I had no foundation on which to build our relationship. We did not even have a common purpose for being in the relationship. He could go for a week without talking to me at all. But when we were in public, people thought we were so in love and I pretended to be happy.

From the day I announced my pregnancy, our lives changed. Tension started building and there were more lies and deceit. Timothy started staying at work until late and spending Saturdays with his Indian friend from school named Laila.

One day as we were coming back from my office Christmas party, Timothy seemed preoccupied.

'When invited to Christmas parties,' he began, 'is it necessary to bring your partner, as in your spouse or girlfriend?'

'No, you don't have to,' I replied.

'So you can bring your sister, brother, niece, nephew, and so on?'

'Yes,' I answered and gave no further thought to the conversation.

The following day he phoned me at work.

'I have something I need to tell you but I don't know where to start,' he said. 'Since I know you are very emotional right now due to the pregnancy, maybe I shouldn't tell you because you are going to cry on me.'

'I think you should just tell me now since you managed to pick up the phone,' I said.

'Well, our Christmas party here at work is on Friday and I wanted to tell you that I am not taking you with me to the party. You see, your pregnancy will be an embarrassment to me. Nobody at work knows you are pregnant and since we are not married yet, it will be embarrassing and irresponsible to show up with you at the function. I thought of taking my younger sister with me but she refused because she said she didn't want to upset you. I was thinking maybe you could find me one of your friends to go with me, someone you trust like your good friend Gladys. Yes, why don't you speak to Gladys about it? We could try your cousin

Reneilwe but since she is very shy, I don't think I would enjoy the evening in her company. Phone Gladys and tell me what she says.'

I felt sick. I could feel the baby move. There I was, listening to my boyfriend, the father of the child I was carrying, the man I slept with every night and cooked for, cleaned for, prepared his work clothes, the man who I had forgiven so many times for all the wrongs he had done, and he was telling me that he thought of me as an embarrassment.

I took a deep breath.

'Why would you be ashamed of me? Are you doing things for your colleagues or for yourself? If you do not want to go with me that's fine. As for Gladys, I am not sure if she will agree to that; she is not stupid. Your colleagues know me anyway, but like I said, you can do what you want.'

I hung up and rushed to the bathroom.

After work I was giving Tim's younger sister a lift home as usual, and I broached the subject with her.

'Tiny, why did you refuse to go with your brother to his work Christmas party next week?'

Tiny said she had not refused. 'Tim never asked me. You know me, I would never say no to something like that. All I know is that he told me he was looking for a date for the Christmas function and when I asked him why he was not taking you he said nothing. And that was the last time we talked about it.'

When we were alone that night I questioned him.

He was angry.

'I did not think you would bring Tiny into this. It was not necessary for you to ask her. Anyway, since you do not want me to go, I won't. I will not even go to work on the day because you are making such a big deal out of this.'

On the day of the Christmas party, I left for work and didn't mention the function. Tim phoned me and said he had not gone into work to avoid being questioned by his manager as to why he

119

was not attending the party. I told him it had nothing to do with me and I had nothing to say.

Things were going from bad to worse but I told myself it must be the pregnancy; maybe he didn't know how to react to it or he couldn't handle it.

Two weeks later, I was attending a workshop and got an urgent message to call my gynaecologist. When I phoned the doctor, I was told I needed to get to the clinic quickly because the blood test they had done the previous week showed that the baby had a high chance of being born with Down's Syndrome. They needed to perform an amniocentesis to check and as I could not drive after the procedure I should come with someone.

I phoned Tim to tell him the news, trying to explain in simple terms that the baby might be abnormal and that I would have to lie down for at least twelve hours after the test as the chances of miscarriage were high. I had expected some sympathy and concern from him but instead he said: 'Why don't you call one of your friends to go with you? I'm busy and I can't come with you.'

I finally went to the clinic with Gladys and Ntombi. Gladys had never been angry about my decision to move in with Tim, and now Ntombi had made peace with the fact that I wanted to work on my relationship with him. Both of my friends had vowed they would support me no matter what happened. Along with the tension in the house, I was even more terrified now because I knew that if my baby did have Down's Syndrome, I would have to care for him or her all by myself. I hoped that the explanation someone had given me about expectant fathers was correct. One of my work colleagues had said that men went into a state of shock when they first heard they were going to be fathers.

Ntombi and Gladys held a vigil for me while the doctors performed the amniocentesis. After the test, Ntombi took me to her house so that I could rest. She was very angry with Tim's lack of support but she was not going to say anything to upset me any further. In the evening Ntombi and her husband drove me home. Tim was not there when I arrived. When he finally came home, he did not ask me anything about the events of the day or my emergency trip to the clinic. It was never discussed at all.

Fortunately, the results of the amniocentesis were negative for Down's Syndrome. The first blood tests the doctor had run, which showed a high risk for Down's Syndrome, had not been accurate.

It was becoming obvious to me that Tim and I had reached a point of no return in our relationship. It was time for action although I was not yet ready to do anything. I did, however, inadvertently help Tim to execute his 'exit strategy'. After two months of tension and stress, no communication, no talk about the baby and no sign of improvement in the situation, things came to a head.

It was a Saturday morning and I was lying in bed feeling sick. For some time now, Tim had been hiding his cellphone away, and he had specifically told me not to answer his phone. He even took it into the bathroom with him. If he left it behind, he would make sure it was off. He knew I no longer knew his pin code so I could not switch it on.

On this day, however, he had been careless. His phone rang and though I did not answer, I saw my opportunity. I ignored the missed call and first scrolled to the calendar to see if the reminder I had put in earlier in the year for my birthday was still there. It was. Then I checked his text messages.

There was only one message, four days old, and I recognised the number as that of the woman I had once found him in the house with. She was giving him her bank details and I guessed Timothy was sending her money to come and visit him again.

I used the phone to call her and she answered with enthusiasm until she heard it was me and not Tim on the other end.

'I want to ask you woman to woman, why are you sending Timothy your banking details? What are you two still doing?'

'Don't ask me stupid questions,' she replied. 'What I do with Timothy is none of your business. And while we are at it, I must tell you that I am not happy because you have hurt me so much by continuing with Timothy. You are now even using his phone and he has told me how much you are making him unhappy and miserable. However, he is mine and I will wait for him to come back to me even if it takes ten years.'

I hung up, picked up my own phone and went outside to call a friend and ask for her advice. I did not know whether to be angry or feel stupid and guilty for what I had done. My friend made me feel worse by giving me the third degree about snooping into Tim's phone when I was pregnant and meant to be avoiding stress. Then I thought of the one person who might be able to help me through the sorry saga. I phoned Dr Gijima and left an urgent message for her.

I went back into the house to tell Timothy what had happened. He would probably reprimand me but I would certainly demand an apology from him. This time he had outdone himself. But there was no opportunity to say anything. As I walked through the kitchen door towards the lounge, Tim was on the phone with someone.

'Don't worry, Tiny, I was expecting it anyway. I have known for a long time that I am living with an insane person. I will sort it out. You phone Thandi and tell her what I said.' He stood up, walked straight past me, got into his car and drove away.

I tried to make sense of what I had heard him say. Thandi was the woman I had just spoken to on the phone, and Tim was now discussing what had happened with his younger sister Tiny. Apparently, Thandi had called Tiny to tell her about the phone call she received from me.

I had terrible stomach pain and diarrhoea for the rest of the day. I was overwhelmed by what had happened and spent the whole day feeling frustrated and confused, angry and hurt and unsure of myself. Later in the evening Tim walked in, went straight to the bedroom, packed a bag and left without a word. That was it, I had made him angry.

Dr Gijima returned my call and we spoke about the incident. I realised I had no reason to feel guilty. I knew it was wrong to snoop and I did not think I should have called Thandi. But I had no reason to apologise at all. I needed to take charge of myself, especially now that I was expecting a baby.

Timothy came home the following evening, Sunday, because he had to go to work the next day. He continued to ignore me and since I had already spoken to Dr Gijima, who told me not to apologise at all and not to allow myself to get dragged into a guilt-ridden argument, I ignored him as well. That evening, I tried to put into practice all the things I had learned from previous therapy sessions. I distanced myself from the situation and decided that if Tim wanted me to say anything he would ask me and I would not allow him to make me feel guilty.

Though we shared the same bed, it was in silence and the following day I called him at work.

'I want to tell you what happened on Saturday morning while you were in the bathroom.' I told him everything and finished: 'That is all I have to say and I thought you should know what I did and thank you for listening.'

'You sound like you are reading a written speech. I wonder who prepared it for you? Have you been talking to your shrink again? Or did you use the advice from all those relationship-fixing books you keep reading? Even better, did you use your Psychology text-books? I must be a nice case study to discuss with your learned friends,' he said sarcastically.

'That is all I called you for and you can think what you want but do not expect anything from me at all. At least you know how I feel, so goodbye.'

I put the phone down and for the first time in three years of terror and guilt, I felt good about myself. I was not going to be dragged into any more games. I had obviously already mourned the end of the relationship because I was amazed at how quickly from that day on I managed to detach myself from it completely. Everything was now about my baby and me and I was not going to be part of any more emotional abuse.

For the whole week we did not talk to each other at all. Tim's younger sister was with us and she kept Tim company while I had my unborn baby to talk to. I also had my therapist, my friends and Tim's elder brother for support, so I was not lonely. This time was different. Previously I had distanced myself from my family and friends when the tension grew between Tim and I. Now I broke the silence because I told my friends the truth about the entire relationship. Although I was still not comfortable trusting other people, at least I knew I was not looking for their sympathy but merely for a friendly ear. I was way past the stage of looking for sympathy.

I cooked and sang in the house while I ignored Tim and Tiny and told myself I would eventually find a way to the final point. I was in no hurry to run away or think about what was going to happen the next day. I took one day at a time, one step at a time. That Friday Tim did not come home and on Saturday morning Tiny came to the bedroom and told me he had asked her to pack all his clothes into a suitcase because he was leaving. At first I told Tiny to get out of the room but then relented and told her to carry on.

Half an hour later he came in and they both got into the car and left. In the evening I had a moment of weakness. I phoned him to ask where he was.

'Oh, you still think I am with another woman? You are so insecure it disgusts me. And let me tell you something, when I

124

come back from where I am going, I will sort you out in five minutes. This time I won't even go with you to your therapist. I will show you who I really am. You will regret phoning Thandi. You are such an embarrassment – I had to call her family and apologise for your behaviour. I explained your insanity to them and at least they understood. But I am not done with you. You must know that I do not run a maternity ward in my house so when I come back the maternity services will be over. I am so sick of your insecurities; I don't think anyone will help you. Not even your therapist can help. I think you were injected with insecurity blood in your system when you were born.'

Quietly I hung up, tears rolling down my cheeks. I was with one of my friends from university days. I had to explain to him why I was crying. My diarrhoea started again and I went to the clinic to get something to stop it. Tim was gone for the remaining weeks of the December holidays without any contact but a friend of mine came to stay and Tiny was there with us.

I had problems over the holidays: I was bleeding, I had ongoing diarrhoea and I feared my baby was going to die. I prayed and made bargains with God, telling Him that if He protected my unborn child I would never stop praying to Him but if He did not, I would never go to church again. During my struggles to deal with the pain I had decided to go back to the local Born Again church. Tim had occasionally even accompanied me. I was still searching for a Saviour other than Tim.

When Tim returned things were no better. After his first day back at work, he gave me an envelope, which contained a formal, typed letter:

28 Tin Avenue
Bloubersrand
Randburg
29 December

Attention: Miss Kedibone
Delivery: By hand

Re: Notice of termination of our agreement

I wish to inform you that your continued violation of my right to privacy and confidentiality, and probably that of other housemates, has reached a point where it can no longer be tolerated. I truly believe that the only remedy for this problem is for you to vacate the property located at the above address as soon as possible.

I therefore have no other alternative at my disposal but to give you notice to vacate the property by no later than the 31st of January. However, should it not be possible for you to find alternative accommodation by the end of January, the notice period may be extended by a further fifteen days which will start from the 1st of February to the 15th of February. Unless you inform the writer of this letter in writing that you require the proposed extension of the notice period, it will be assumed that there is no need to extend the notice period.

I should also advise you to ensure that all your assets have been removed from this property by the last day of the notice period since your access to the property will no longer be available as from the first day after the expiry of the notice period.

Yours sincerely,
Timothy Mhleli Msimango

While I was reading the letter, Tim lay on the couch having a conversation with someone on the phone, pretending not to care. I had to rush to the bathroom. My diarrhoea was so bad I felt like the baby was about to come out. I stayed in the bathroom for a while and prayed for strength. Then I went outside to call Dr Gijima. She was shocked and advised me to move out as soon as possible. I did not know whether to call my mother or not, but I still did not want her to know how much I was failing. I called Ntombi and Gladys.

That evening, Tim moved into the other bedroom and avoided me whenever possible. In the morning I called work and reported I was not feeling well. I phoned Tim's elder brother to see if he would be willing to talk some sense into Tim. He was appalled by Tim's actions but since he was far away, he gave me their aunt's number. He thought she might help and he also thought I needed to speak to a woman because she would know how to handle such things. I drove to my friend's house and slept the whole day. Later I went to see Tim's aunt who promised to speak to him. Evidently she did, for Tim became very angry with me, telling me that since I was not married to him, I had no right to involve his family in my insecurities. He told me never to speak to his aunt again.

He did not want to be in the same room as me and would wait until I left for work to get his clothes from the bedroom. He only came home after I had gone to bed. Each time I saw him my diarrhoea would start and I was told by my doctors that if I stayed in the house any longer, I might have a miscarriage and my baby might die. All I wanted was for my baby to survive. I began to panic and tried to get Tim to discuss the problem but he refused, saying we would only talk when I had left the house. He said I shouldn't take long with my response to his letter and it should be in writing.

One day when I came home from work I found a stopper on the lock and could not get into the house. When I phoned him, he told me: 'I will come when I want and by the way remember that from the 1st of February your access to the house will be taken away.'

The day after that, I asked if we could at least be civil and talk about the situation. I wanted us to discuss the pregnancy and the baby before I moved out. I also asked for more time to find suitable accommodation. It was clear to me that there was nothing I could do to fix the problem and I had progressed from feeling betrayal to loss, a loss of myself and of him. I ate alone, slept alone and on the day he agreed to talk, he became even more abusive than he had been before.

When I told him I could not move out that quickly when I was pregnant, he said: 'Why don't you go and stay with your learned friends? I am sure I have now became a suitable case study for you to enhance your knowledge of Psychology even more. You all think you are so smart. I am sure your degrees will help you to manage. Your friends must think you are an angel. You are not, you are a manipulative little thing and I even suspect you were abused as a child and your parents didn't know about it. I have reached a point where I cannot discuss anything with you while you are still in the house. If you think you can use this pregnancy to get what you want out of me, you are wrong. Some men have kids all over the country and they were never forced to stay with the mothers. Why should I be forced to stay with you? If you are trying to prolong your stay here in the hope that things will get better, you are very wrong. I can't stand you, not even for an hour, and how do you expect me to let it go on? Every day when I come home from work, I pray to God that I will not find you here. Why are your rich friends not giving you a place to stay?'

'I don't think it would be appropriate for me to burden them while I am pregnant,' I replied. 'What if something goes wrong with me or the baby?'

Tim was not sympathetic to my pleas at all.

'What makes you think that if you continue to stay here, you and that thing will survive?' he said. 'Do you think I even care about what happens to you? The more that thing grows inside you, the more you disgust me. And you still think I should have mercy for you. You can pray all you want. For that matter even your praying disgusts me. I just want you out of here. I am running out of time. I have even bought replacements of all the things that belong to you. So I need my bedroom back and all my space. I want my freedom back. If money is a problem and seeing that you are going to experience financial problems when you leave here because of the pregnancy, maybe I should bid for your satellite dish. The money would help you.'

I could not answer. I ran to the toilet. I was beginning to hate being pregnant. I did not want the baby any more but I was in a dilemma. I could not abort it and I could not kill myself. I was lonely and frightened inside. That night was the first time that I understood the meaning of the song by the group Madodana A se Wesele 'Lala ho nna shwelane e wele' ('Abide with me since the dusk has cracked'). I put the CD on, knelt next to the bed and said, 'Oh dear God, if you are up there and listening, please take care of my baby while I take care of the father. Give me strength to deal with him. All I want from you is to take care of my baby.' It was as honest and desperate a plea as I could make. When I woke up later in the night I realised that I had not switched off the music. The CD was now on the track 'Lala honna'. All I heard was 'Wena ya sa feteng lala ho nna' ('Abide with me the one that never leaves; please abide with me when the night falls'). I felt confused and guilty that an innocent child was involved in the mess of my relationship with Timothy.

I did not know whether to call my mother or not. She knew I was pregnant but she had no idea I was living with Tim. She had also never asked me any details about my life or the baby's father. I did not know what I would say to her. I thought of my aunt in

Johannesburg but I had seen how angry she was when she had to come to the medical centre the night I had a threatened miscarriage and Timothy was nowhere to be found. She had looked at me with pain in her eyes and not questioned me any further. Timothy and I had visited her a lot until the news of my pregnancy broke. Now I went to visit alone and my aunt never commented on or questioned me about his absence.

In the morning I started to investigate many different forms of advice – legal, social, professional and religious. I asked the pastors at the church to pray for me. My doctor kept warning me about the situation. At first I could not tell him why I was experiencing so much ongoing diarrhoea. I waited until he wanted to hospitalise me before I burst into tears and said: 'I have diarrhoea every time I see my baby's father walk into the house. I can't take this any more and my baby is going to die.'

The doctor told me that if I got diarrhoea again, he would have to admit me to hospital and I was fortunate that I was not yet dehydrated. One of my friends suggested I should go to the police because if Timothy was locking me out, I would struggle to remove my furniture from the house. Two days before I moved out, I went to the police station to report the matter and was told the Domestic Violence Unit would help me. The detective at the police station phoned Tim and asked him to come over so that we could both tell our story. Tim told the detective that he would rather we went and talked to our therapist. He was not prepared to discuss our problems with the police. The he hung up. I had to go home. I found Tim and Tiny watching television. All he said was, 'Oh, now you're thinking your police friends will help you? I am not scared of them at all. I have done nothing wrong. I have sought legal advice and I am doing nothing unlawful at all. This is my house and I can kick and keep anyone I like.' I ignored him and went to bed.

On Wednesday the 17th of January I gave Timothy a response to his letter in which I wrote:

Dear Timothy,

I acknowledge receipt of your letter dated 29th December in which you stated your intentions to terminate our living arrangement. In response to your letter and with reference to the verbal agreement we entered into on the 26th of April 2000 to live together in the same house as boyfriend and girlfriend, I have the following to say:

It was agreed that since I do not own a house, I would be given sufficient time to look for proper accommodation before vacating the property. I would like to bring it to your attention that 30 days is not sufficient time for me to find proper accommodation.

In addition, you are aware that I am pregnant with your child who is due in May 2001. It has been difficult and will continue to be, given the time frame of your notice period, for me to find proper accommodation suitable for bringing up a baby. I therefore request that you extend your extension period to the 30th of April 2001. Another reason for my request is that I will be going on maternity leave from the 1st of May 2001 and I will be in Pietersburg for the period of my leave which is until the 31st of August 2001.

Given the circumstances described above, I will continue to pay my contribution towards the house until the month of my departure as part of my responsibility towards our living arrangements.

Furthermore, since you have made it clear that you want no further communication between the two of us after my departure, I would request that we discuss the baby's maintenance and support before I leave the property.

Yours sincerely,
Kedibone Modiba

Timothy asked Tiny to leave us alone so that we could have some privacy. He read parts of the letter out loud and commented sarcastically as he went along: 'agree', 'disagree', 'well written', 'poor grammar', 'thank you for reminding me about the baby'. 'All in all, it was well written,' he remarked. 'But I will only respond once you are out of here.'

Despite my best efforts, there was no negotiating with him and so the following day I looked for a moving company and booked a truck to come and move my furniture into storage. I went to stay with a colleague. I felt ashamed and guilty that I was going to give birth to a child who would not have a father because I had made him angry. I felt ugly, unwanted and worthless. These feelings, as always, I kept inside myself because I didn't want the world to know I had failed again. It was another load of pain and fear and I became more and more withdrawn from everyone, especially my family. Instead I spoke to total strangers about my problems because I knew I would never see them again.

My therapist asked me to live temporarily with her and I was able to stay there for two weeks before I moved in full-time with another colleague while looking for my own place. I focused only on the pregnancy.

I realised the mistakes I was continuing to make. I wanted to bring an innocent life into my brokenness. I wanted to fulfil my own selfish needs. I wondered how girls and boys are raised and nurtured to become mothers and fathers. Who equipped them to be parents? I was devastated when Dr Gijima moved overseas. We said our goodbyes and she referred me to one of her colleagues, but I could not bear the thought of dealing with someone I did not know. Instead, I focused on the arrival of my baby.

My GP advised me to see someone because I was not coping with the pregnancy and the end of my relationship. I had started visiting the GP a lot because of ongoing pain and headaches. He was aware that I was depressed and he was afraid I was going to strain the baby and complicate the pregnancy. My gynaecologist was also helpful. He listened to me and comforted me all the time. But it was the GP who encouraged me to go back to therapy and deal with all my problems. He had treated me before the pregnancy and was aware of my 'resident depressive episodes'. This time he thought my condition was particularly dangerous since there was a baby on the way. I went to a psychiatrist for evaluation and then was referred to a clinical psychologist who would help me with counselling. But I could only bring myself to go for one session.

11

It was when I gave birth to my son that my world changed and I became a child again. Everything that I had not experienced as a child was happening right in front of me. I was in awe of the role I had to play. Tumi (an abbreviation of Boitumelo – Joy) was tiny and very dark with big eyes. I had the support of all my friends and aunts during his birth and my hospital room was full of flowers and messages wishing us well. My friend Nthabiseng was in the delivery room to play husband and Gladys came to pick us up when we were discharged. Ntombi and her husband made sure I had everything I needed for Tumi. Another friend, Refilwe, with whom I had stayed after moving out of Tim's house, was there to make sure I was happy and well. Even Tim's aunts were pleased with the baby's smooth arrival and my mother was excited to have a new grandchild. No one mentioned Timothy.

The birth of my son was a second chance I was given to claim my happiness and see life differently. I was amazed there were no complications – he was a perfectly healthy and normal baby. I was now entrusted with the responsibility of being someone's mother. Before Tumi's birth, life had been all about fighting to protect myself, my secrets, pain, anger and hurt. I hid away and pretended I had never been through such horrors. I always felt the urge to have things in order and neatly done so that what lay beneath would never be revealed. I vowed to protect my son from the world and to ensure that he never experienced the things I did, and if by some terrible twist of fate he did, then he would not be alone. I would be with him from day one.

I gave birth to a most ugly angel who became the most beautiful instrument that God used to commence my healing. All the awful things happening around the pregnancy and certain passages from the Bible that I had been taught – in particular, Exodus 20: 5–6, '*Ke tla otla bana ka lebaka la bokgopo bja batswadi be bona*' ('I, the Lord your God, am a jealous God, visiting the iniquity of the fathers on the children) – had terrified me and convinced me that my baby would not be normal or that something terrible would happen. But Tumi's uncomplicated arrival and his normal, healthy state proved all my fears to be unfounded. He was not to be punished for anyone's sins. And I was determined to ensure that his father's iniquities would not befall him. I prayed for him every day. Eventually I realised that Tumi came with his own purpose – to live his own life and make his own mistakes. I was frightened when I saw him for the first time because I did not know why I was so confused about the name I had just given him. I had no idea that this child who looked nothing like me was going to have such an impact on my life. I thought my duty was to make sure he would never be hurt and would never live the life I had. I was wrong; it was his purpose to make sure I let go of the pain before I could protect him. He refused to let me contaminate him with my pain; he surprised me the first time I took him home. He never showed any feelings of insecurity; he was forever sure of what he wanted and would scream to get it.

I had mixed feelings when I took Tumi home from the hospital. I was not excited to be a mother. All I could think about was how to make his world a better place. Why couldn't Tim at least come to hold his baby with me in hospital? Though Nthabiseng was with me, I thought that I needed my baby's father. My doctors were worried I was going to have post-natal depression. I did not, but the stress of my life made me unable to breastfeed because I could not produce any milk. Tumi was always hungry because he could not get enough milk from me. The doctor gave me some tablets to help stimulate my milk supply but I did not want my child to drink milk made from tablets.

My mother suggested we buy him formula and he was much happier when he was fed on this from a bottle. I blamed myself for this and worried I could have done better. I thought, if only I had not made his father leave, maybe I would be fit and healthy enough to feed my child. I thought it was all my fault that Tim had left and was convinced that if I were different my son would have his father with him.

It was painful recalling the day Tim had said to me: 'I even suspect you were abused as a child and your parents didn't know about it.'

The more I remembered his words, the guiltier I felt. I had never told him anything about my childhood and so I thought it must be obvious. No wonder no one would ever think of me as a better person. Some days when I was not feeling guilty about his leaving, I wondered if all men were incapable of loving children. If they could love, why did my father leave, why were all my aunts single mothers, along with my sisters and cousins? And now me. If men could love, why did they leave and why was my baby's father not interested in his child? He had kicked me out of the house we shared and told me that he didn't want to see me any more. Remembering all these things terrified me even more. I did not know if I could handle the responsibility of being a mother, let alone be a good one if I was feeling so guilty, ashamed, angry and confused. In my quest to find happiness, I had screwed up things for everyone including my child. Now I was feeling like a child again myself.

Every day I watched Tumi grow. I realised that if I wanted to build a solid foundation for him, I needed to start afresh. The conflict within me meant I was not able to give him a healthy foundation unless I dealt with my own childhood. What about how and where I learned to be a mother?

I thought that maybe if I had had a daughter, I would have known better how to mother her. There I was with a baby boy and all my interactions with men had been dysfunctional and painful. How was I supposed to nurture the relationship with my son when I was now more convinced than ever that men were cruel people who had no emotions? They raped children; they left their families, and they impregnated women and abandoned them. Many girls had to live with the consequences of not knowing how to behave in their male-female relationships. How would I be able to show my son that we could have a healthy and loving relationship when I myself could not deal with my inability to derive love from men? I had to make a decision: either let it be and have an unhealthy relationship or deal with my past and learn how to be a loving and caring mother. These thoughts dominated my mind every time I held my son.

I also knew that one day I would meet a man and my son would have to relate to him as well. How could I facilitate a positive relationship if my view of men was so negative? Along with reviewing my ideas about men, I would have to begin to embrace my mother and family so that my son knew who he was and where he came from. The trouble was, I had long ago given up on forming any relationship with my mother and siblings. I was aloof. For a while I considered isolating my son from the entire family.

I decided to find a lawyer who could contact Timothy to discuss child support. The letter my lawyers sent to Tim read:

Dear Mr Msimango,

<u>Re: Demand for child maintenance</u>

We act on behalf of our client Miss Kedibone Modiba in this matter.

We have been instructed to demand in terms of the Maintenance Act 99 of 1998 the payment of maintenance from yourself for one Tumi Modiba, a child born of Miss Modiba and yourself, you being able to do so and being personally and legally liable to maintain the said child.

In terms of your common law duty to support the said child, this support extends to such support as a child reasonably requires for his proper living and upbringing.

Should you require any further information please contact us at the above number.

To this Tim replied:

Dear Sirs,

<u>Re: Child Maintenance</u>

I acknowledge receipt of your letter and to say the least I am somewhat surprised by the contents thereof.

When your client approached me with the news that she had been diagnosed as having a condition known as endometriosis, she informed me that the gynaecologists at the clinic to which I took her, who made this diagnosis, warned her that the condition was incurable and once it reached an advanced stage it would destroy her ability to conceive and bear children.

139

She therefore pleaded with me that we should have a child immediately so as to fulfil one of her main wishes in life which was to be a mother. After I made it clear to her that I could not afford to have a child for financial reasons, she assured me that she was a professional woman and she would support the child herself. I was convinced she would be financially capable of supporting the child on her own and that I would never be held responsible for maintenance of any nature whatsoever.

Having read your letter it has become clear to me that Miss Modiba's financial circumstances are not as good as she presented them to me before the child was conceived. Since I am also unable to assist with the required maintenance, I therefore respectfully submit that we consider the possibility of giving up the child for adoption in order to protect his interests. Kindly inform your client that unless she informs me of her objection to my submission, I intend to go ahead with a search for potential child adopters.

Yours sincerely,
Mr Msimango

Tim's letter hurt me very much but I still blamed myself. I now knew that while in most cases people do not choose to become single parents, I virtually became a single mother by choice. I chose to stay in the relationship. I was making a choice to give an innocent life my own broken, unhealthy life. In the midst of the loveless relationship with Tim and our vicious circle of abuse and manipulation of each other's circumstances and events, I still saw fit to bring a baby into the equation. Ours was not a relationship built on love and commitment; it was built on a broken foundation and lies. On my side, it was ruled by insecurities and fears of abandonment.

I went to court for the application after realising we were not going to reach any sort of understanding. It was evident from Tim's letter that I was on my own. In the midst of the court case, the news that Tim was marrying a woman who had a child by another man shook me. I became more determined to protect my son because I thought if his father was marrying another woman with a child, then it was my son he didn't want. If it wasn't about my son, then wouldn't he at least show an interest in him – or, when he married, wouldn't he marry someone without a child? The bottom line was that Tim did not want *my* child. My days were spent in court: Tim removed Tumi from his medical aid without telling me; he did not buy the clothes he had promised to provide, and for six months he failed to pay any maintenance. I vowed that Tumi would be taken care of but not in the midst of all the anger, frustrations and garbage that existed through no fault of his own.

In order to fight for Tumi's rights to a better life in a fair manner, I had to bury the dead and know that when I stood up in front of the court, my past did not jeopardise my son's interests. I did not want the case to bring back emotions from the past that would make me look like a failure again. I could not continue to strive to be a good mother with all the conflicts that existed inside of me: the conflicts about why my father left, why I was raped twice, why I became a single mother and why I could not give my son a home with two parents. During the course of the court trips, the disrespectful treatment I received from Timothy did not help the situation. I was becoming more and more humiliated and hurt each time I had an encounter with him. I felt pity for Tumi each time he looked up and smiled at me. Finally, I wrote Timothy a letter that, although I never posted it, helped to set me free:

Dear Timothy,

For the past week you have done nothing but upset me every time you get an opportunity and I keep asking myself if it was necessary for you to do that. You might be thinking less of me now but I am still the mother of your son and for that you should be grateful. The one thing I ask myself is, how do you expect your son to respect and love you if you cannot respect his mother? Children protect the people who love and look after them and you might not think about it now, but my son will not appreciate anyone who disrespects and ill-treats his mother. It takes more than honouring a court order to be a father to someone.

As for me, you may think and say what you want about me, but one thing is sure, you can never wipe the fact that I am his mother and I am the one who will see him through bad and hard times. I have learned to make peace with you and let go of you. I respect your wish to live a separate life away from me but Tumi's existence gives us a common ground. Your angry tantrums are not helping the situation but worsening it. As a mother, I will do everything with God's help to protect this baby even if it means putting my life at risk.

I am writing this letter to forgive you for all the horrible things you said to me. I forgive you for not being honest with me, for lying to me when you always wanted things to go your way. I forgive you for abusing me verbally and emotionally when you did not talk to me for a month and when you did, you said so many horrible things to me. I forgive you for trying to convince yourself that you were the only one doing the best that you could for our relationship. I forgive you for kicking me out on the streets and telling me you wanted to throw me out of the gate without opening it so that my cousin Reneilwe could come with the runaway car to pick me up. I forgive you for the night you wanted to bring another woman in the house when you thought I went away to visit my mother. I don't know why it happened but I forgive you for all the women you slept with while we were together. I forgive you for thinking that I used my pregnancy to get what I wanted. I forgive you for never telling me you had a problem with me being pregnant but just started treating me badly. I forgive you for telling me you do not run a maternity ward in your house and calling me a liar and a manipulator and yet you knew I never tricked you into anything against your will. I forgive you for saying that I am worse than your ex and yet you know the truth. I forgive you for knowing the truth and not wanting to accept it. I forgive you for all the lies you told about me. I forgive you for rejecting my son.

Before I go, I want to thank you for the times I thought you loved me so much you would do anything to keep our relationship. Thank you for creating such a beautiful baby boy with me. It is your choice to become a father to this baby and to provide the amount of support needed financially, emotionally and mentally. You are under no obligation to perform the last two but God knows financially you will have to comply. Trust me, God entrusted this child's survival to me because I am his mother and for that I will do the right thing even if you never talk to me again. If you want nothing to do with your child, it is your choice but please learn to respect me at least as your fellow human being. I will no longer tolerate your abusive treatment. I want you to know that we will spend as much time as it takes in court until my child gets what he rightfully deserves. As for me, since you have managed to strip off every shred of security I had left in my system, I will never ever embrace you again. You made *me lose all that I have fought for many years to sustain: my self-worth and my purpose in life. I will never allow myself to relive that pain again. Hence I am releasing you.*

Goodbye

While trying to deal with the difficulties of single parenting and my battle for child support, the treatment I received from the court meant I had to fight even harder for my child. The justice system seemed to favour Tim. He defaulted on several occasions; he did not honour his promises, and our case was continually postponed. We would spend the whole day in court for nothing. Timothy had himself surrounded by attorneys who managed to intimidate the maintenance officer, while I had no money and represented myself.

When I finally got the maintenance order forcing Tim to pay, he continued to default and disrespect the order, particularly after he was married. But with perseverance and courage, I managed to get him jailed for his defaulting. I did not want to start any new relationships until my life had been sorted out and I wanted my son to be free to establish relationships with males without being prejudiced by my experiences. The justice system had managed to get Tim to perform his parental obligations. I was not going to give up.

My fight for Tumi's rights became part of my acknowledgement of my past choices and I had to go through all these exercises as part of my renewal process. My GP was helping me take things one step at a time without feeling guilty. Although I had someone to look after Tumi while I was at work, I still had problems coping with everything around me and I suffered from bouts of depression. I felt that I was nowhere near a personal victory.

12

Two years later, I was lying in a bed in the psychiatric ward of a private hospital after my therapy session with the clinical psychologist. I had been admitted and was being observed and helped by a three-person team consisting of a psychiatrist, a clinical psychologist and an occupational therapist. I was very depressed and scared, scared that this time around I really was going to die because I could no longer face the things that kept bubbling to the surface. In my dazed state, I believed that what I had endured in my life to date, I would continue to endure for as long as I lived. But the birth of my son made it difficult for me to embrace that fate.

It had become a vicious circle. One year I would be content with myself and everything around me and would be able to hide my pain. Then something would come along that would be the catalyst for everything to start flooding back.

My body mirrored my troubled mental state. Every time I felt threatened, I would suffer from infections, flu and body pains that I could not attribute to anything. I was constantly struggling with hay fever and my sleeping pattern had deteriorated. The panic attacks had returned even more fiercely.

I had reached a dead end in my journey. Since I had stopped seeing Dr Gijima, I had not dealt with my issues appropriately.

Lying there in my hospital bed, I thought of Tumi who depended on my sanity and good health, who needed me to provide for his welfare and protect him from the wrath of my past. There was no way I could continue to ignore my past or my current problems.

What had caused my most recent pain was that I could no longer keep Tumi with me because I was feeling too ill and my financial situation made it difficult for me to afford a minder for him. I had to send him to live at my mother's place, which was a three-hour drive away. This meant I could only see him every two months because it was expensive to travel there.

It was the first time we had been separated since his birth and I felt such pain when I left him. He cried very hard as I drove away because he did not have a real relationship with my family – to Tumi his family was me, the nanny and my three good friends, Lerato, Nthabiseng and Gladys.

My situation at work was also abysmal. The more I went in, the sicker I became. I had no joy, no challenge, no feeling of being appreciated and I had lost confidence in my abilities. My doctor felt it was damaging for me to continue to go to work – I had spent almost ten months doing nothing that I enjoyed, and often having nothing to do at all. My will to wake up and face the day was dead.

Two months previously, I had received a summons from the bank that they would repossess my house if I did not make up the payments I had missed when I was on maternity leave. The arrears had accumulated interest along with those payments that I had skipped when I could not afford them, and so I was behind with everything: the car payments, the levies, the electricity bill and the doctors' accounts during and after Tumi's birth. I was sinking further into debt and the money Tim was paying for child support was too little to cover all the costs. I had to pay for the child minder, buy food for Tumi, pay his medical bills and maintain myself – all from my own income.

A week after I took Tumi to my mother's, my electricity was cut off and I became so ill that I was admitted to hospital. I was grateful for my friends. Even though they thought the root of my collapse was my financial situation and my work environment, they came through for me and gave me their support.

My doctors were the only people who knew what the real issues were. Since the previous December, I had been feeling completely uneasy, detached from myself and not liking where I was. Then in January, I became very ill after I heard that a friend's husband had passed away. I did not understand how his death could affect me so much. I was often short of breath and cried a lot. My body was failing me and when I arrived in hospital, I was told that my immune system had been weakened by my constant worries and the many things I had kept inside for so long.

As I lay there thinking about my therapy session, I came to see that my views on life were all too often based on projections in which I feared someone might do something to me or that something would happen to me. I frequently thought that people didn't like me or disapproved of me and that way of thinking paralysed me from becoming aware of my perspectives and as-sumptions, and prevented me from gaining freedom from my own fears, pain and problems.

My depression was a constant, something I had walked through all the phases of my life with. My achievements, failures, joys and sorrows all happened with me hiding behind a smiling mask I presented to the world. Known only to myself, I would now and again have a depressive episode and no one would notice except for my GP when I saw him for headache pills. I would usually get better depending on what was going on in my life at the time. My doctor had asked me after I gave birth to consider being treated for my depression but I refused.

This time I had no choice; I was becoming something I could not handle. I had been too sick too often and my energies were spent on trying to get better while I neglected other aspects of my life. My financial situation was not the main problem because I knew I could lose material belongings and then gather them again. My situation at work was not the issue either. I could quit at any time. In fact, my doctor and those around me thought I should leave my job because I was no longer valued and had not enjoyed myself since my mentor Peter Kennedy had retired.

Though I had been admitted to the very same hospital and ward six years previously, then I had managed to escape without touching on the real reasons why I suffered from so many terrible headaches and could no longer cope at work. On that occasion, the doctors dealt only with my headaches and did not bother me with any therapy sessions. After all, I had only gone there because of the tension headaches I was suffering from.

For the two years prior to my current admission, I had managed to avoid the hospital and instead ended up on the therapist's couch. With Dr Gijima I had unravelled the root of my problems but there had been no time to move on to the solutions. When she left the country I never made a serious commitment to continue therapy with the other doctors to whom I was referred. The thought of starting from the very beginning again had been too awful to contemplate and I convinced myself that because I had at least told someone, I could simply carry on as if it no longer mattered.

Lying in hospital now forced me to confront all the hidden things that had turned me into a silent child who kept drawing strength by withdrawing to a private world. I needed to ask myself a lot of questions, the answers to which would inevitably lead me to undesirable places. Why was I continuously scared? What did I do wrong? Who sent those people to hurt me? Who would rescue me? Who exactly was the ideal me? How had I managed to live to this far? Where did I find the courage? What were the changes in behaviour that should I make? Did I need to apologise to anyone for being who I am? Could I move forward?

My frequent therapy sessions were forcing me to begin the healing process by answering these and many other questions. I was determined to do it, even though my fears were sometimes overwhelming.

13

A long with trying to deal with my past and embrace motherhood, I realised the importance of establishing a relationship with my mother, the woman I had hated in silence for too long. I finally wrote to her, sending her a long account of all the things I had been through in my life and how much I thought she had failed me. Apart from anything else, I could not understand why I had been given the name Kedibone, meaning 'I have seen enough'. To me, as the saying goes in Sepedi, *'leina lebe ke seromo'* (a bad name is a curse). Her lengthy response to my letter surprised me and it was a significant step in my healing process to reply to her now that I understood how we felt about each other.

Dear Mother,

I was surprised by your thirteen-page response to my story. Your letter thanked me for my story and the fact that its contents have given you a light as to why I have never liked you, why I have always treated you like a stranger in my life and not like a mother, why we have never had the mother-daughter friendship that many women do. For me, the most important part of your letter was when you responded to my asking why I was given the name 'Kedibone'. Now I would like to tell you how I have always felt about my name.

To me, and in our culture, names have meanings. You named me Kedibone and every time you called my name, you were saying to me and to the world 'I have seen enough'. You could have called me Tebogo or Mpho but I have to live with the name Kedibone. Do you know how many questions and gazes I get from people when they hear my name? I resent my name for it is not a reminder of the joy you experienced when I was born.

I've always wanted to know why you called me Kedibone and finally in your letter you've answered my question. Do you realise that I was made to carry the burden of your silence and your inability to act when you were wrongfully accused of adultery by my father?

You said in your letter, 'your name came to me when you were born because your father had rejected my pregnancy. He had ill-treated me such that my uncle had to remove me from his family where he had left me with his mother and sisters who took all the money he would send. When you were born, I had to stay in the hospital to wait for the doctors to run DNA tests to prove to your father that you were his child. Even after the tests were positive, he still did not believe it and he did not want to take me back.' While I understand your pain, mother, I want to know if you for a moment even imagined the trauma such a name would bring to my life? Did it bother you or was I just an instrument for you to exhale your pain? Did you hate your husband so much and were you so powerless that I was the only one to offer you some form of retaliation? A retaliation contained in the name you chose for me.

You separated from my father after I was born. You moved away from him physically and mentally. But you still carried your frustration and anger. Every time you called me you were actually telling my father and his family that you had had enough of them. Do you realise that even once you no longer needed to tell them that you had had enough of their ill-treatment, I have still carried the name Kedibone? Has it never occurred to you that maybe when your burden eased, you could have changed my name?

Along with the name, I carry with me all sorts of emotions towards you, my father and our whole community – anger, emptiness, fear and confusion. I cannot believe no one was there to stop you from giving me such a name. In your letter, you talk about how unsurprised people were when you told them the name you had given me. You say they knew what you went through because you were the talk of the whole village. Until now I have continued with your legacy mother, the legacy of silence and voicelessness. But I find it difficult to keep it up any longer, now that I am a mother myself.

In your letter you also said, 'thank you for blaming me for your so-called daddy's disappearance. Why didn't you ask me if you had questions?' You know very well that I was not allowed to ask you, an elder, about things like these. They were things that only adults knew about and children could not ask questions about. You talk about your mother-in-law and her daughter's inability to help you, how much they rejoiced in your pain, telling you that it was not their place to interfere but if their son and brother did not want you, you would be made to leave. Could it be that you also watched to see how much and how far I would fight to become a woman?

You said, 'I knew about your sufferings. I knew that you were not a happy child.' But how could you turn a blind eye when you could have protected me?

Now that I am privileged to be a mother myself I have

difficulty understanding why you turned a blind eye in the face of my traumas. You mentioned that I caused you so much pain, that you lost the community's respect because of me, how much your health suffered because of my rebellion. You waited for me to feel the pain I made you feel. You made me believe from the night that I called for your help when Bra Joe was raping me that it was all a bad dream. You never even checked my genitals to see if it was real. I had to hide my pain because it was all a bad dream to you and it would be to the rest of the community if I had spoken about it outside our home. Being a woman, you knew exactly what had happened that night. You knew your limitations, your inability to confront Bra Joe, just like you could not confront your husband and his family. You knew how scandalous it would be if it was known to the community that your daughter was just like other girls.

Mother, I am writing to you because as a mother myself, I remember the saying 'mmago ngwana o tshwara thipa ka bogaleng' (a child's mother holds the knife by its blade). I am holding that knife by its blade for my child's sake. I can no longer see the world through your eyes. I cannot hide behind what can be spoken of and what cannot. That is something that killed some of my friends and loved ones and no one, especially the mothers, could do anything about it. You wanted me to ignore what was happening around me and to me. The Bra Joe incident was not the first time that my body was invaded by a man, but you were not there to protect me and comfort me through the pain. On that night with Bra Joe, I recalled the familiar breathing, the fluids and confusion. That night, mother, you could have given me and yourself the opportunity to break the silence. But instead, you trapped me in silence as well. I kept quiet just as you told me – 'a bad dream'.

I was surprised by the doctor's reaction when I got to university and went to see a doctor for the first time about my vaginal itchiness and discharge. The itching and discharge had been a part of me for as long as I could remember. The doctor said that these vaginal infections only happened to people who were sexually active. He told me I could not have had them for such a long time unless I had been sexually active from an early age.

Yes, I carried them for a long time and I could not share my problems with you at all. It was just a bad dream, or something that girls go through when they grow up. Just like when I experienced terrible abdominal pains with my periods. All I got from you was, 'It is part of being a woman'.

Today I want to tell you about the difference between you, both my paternal and maternal grandmothers, and myself. My silence then was self-imposed out of fear as well as from the voicelessness of a powerless child. You let it happen to me just like your mother and your in-laws let things happen to you in the name of 'lebitla la mosadi ke bogadi' (a woman's grave is at her in-laws' home). There are probably a lot of things that happened to girls during your time that I will never know about. Your many secrets and experiences are protected by sayings such as 'koma re bolla kgororwane, khupamarama re hwa nayo' (we only reveal a little and secrecy we take with us to the grave). Something you said in your letter made me realise you were very much aware of what happened to girls. You ended by saying, 'There are certain things about our relationship that I am not prepared to reveal to you. I will take them with me to the grave.' In my soul and spirit, I do not have a problem with that. You can take as much as you want with you to the grave. But I will not continue to suffer because things are 'a bad dream', because I'm 'just a spoilt girl looking for attention', 'a naughty girl'.

I respect your decisions and actions and I free you to do what suits you. But what I know and what I have seen, I will tell. Things happened to me and to other girls right in front of me. By silencing me, you let it happen to me and others, but I cannot let it happen to the daughters of the world, the daughters I might have. I will never tell them it was a bad dream. I will no longer be made to believe it was a bad dream. I have written to you and to the women before you to liberate myself.

Along with the courage I have found to give myself a voice, I have decided to stop using the name 'Kedibone'. I have found the strength to want to leave a different legacy for my children, both girls and boys. I know that my ancestors will forgive me for what I have said. I am in any case supposed to continue as their descendant to build a community of strong women in our clan. I know that some pains are universal but I don't think that if it was acceptable for you to suffer, it would be acceptable for me as well.

I continue to respect my culture and tradition and in doing that I honour you and those women before you. I acknowledge the struggles women face under the cultural customs of respect your husband; never talk back to your husband; suffer and listen to your husband; your husband's family comes first; if they are not pleased with you, you cannot continue to be in their son's life. I am liberating myself from those and other sayings that keep women prisoners. I hope one day when I get married, I will be treated as an equal by my husband.

Today I want to give up your pain and the burden of the name that you gave me. I can no longer carry it any more. It was too much for me to carry and it will be too much for my children to handle. You and I can go back to that special place we had before you gave me the name – the time when I

156

was kicking in your womb. You wanted me to be perfect and rescue you from your world. And I did, since you used to call me your 'little angel in the blue train'. I was the apple of your eye but then you turned a blind eye on that apple. I cannot be the child you expected me to be but I am the woman I was meant to be when I came into this world.

And now, in defence of my womanhood and motherhood, I want us to start afresh. I hope it is not too late for us to find each other.

Your dearest daughter

14

Wrong conditions of life can be turned into false beliefs and your belief system can be totally confused because of the conditions in your life. When I examined my past, I realised that what I witnessed and experienced was integrated into my definition of who I was. As a child, I had no understanding of how my world and the conditions of my upbringing affected me at a deeper level. I only woke up when I held my own child in my arms. I could not sow the seeds of my anger and resentment into his life. I had to start afresh by letting go of my mother and father's world and its silent teachings before I could become a mother to my son, and by accepting the responsibility for my own thinking, deeds and behaviour from when I was a child to the day I became a mother.

I realised I could not remain a little girl any more or continue as a powerless and helpless adult seeking to please and appease everyone. Whether you have healthy beginnings or slaughtered ones, it makes no difference. You have to grow and become a responsible and capable citizen. I decided to affirm my rights as a woman and an adult. To do this, I had to appreciate all my past experiences and my mother, and stop allowing all the situations in my life to provoke the same old reactions in me. I could no longer separate my feelings from my life. I had to learn to acknowledge them and deal with them.

Every day, I try to learn something new, accept my experiences and more fully understand myself and my place in the world and universe. My aim is to grow old with no regrets. I no longer allow my past to ruin my interactions with people. I have redefined the way I relate to and interact with people. I have formed new relationships, revived old valuable ones, discarded unwanted ones and I maintain the good ones I already had.

Sometimes it is tough and for that reason I have decided to stay in therapy for as long as it takes to help me on those days when I feel like falling back into my old patterns. I still have momentary lapses but at least I now know how to acknowledge them and admit that I am not perfect. On those days when I feel alone and frightened, I remind myself of where I come from and where I am going. I also know that I will have to continue to seek refuge and support from those who love and care for me.

I have stopped worrying that my deepest darkest pains will come out and haunt me or be known by uncaring people. Now that I have acknowledged them all by myself, I have no fear. I no longer feel alone in the world. I have my child, my family, my friends and acquaintances.

I watch Tumi every day and know I made the right choice by having him and not staying with his father. I know my son loves me unconditionally and it is an expansion of all the love I have received but have never acknowledged or recognised. I have never seen anyone love someone like Tumi loves me. He sees me as his mother and that is enough. I know I have a responsibility to love him and teach him to be a better person.

I have also accepted that Timothy decided not to be involved in his son's life by choice, not because of me or Tumi. I stopped blaming myself and feeling sorry for my son. Interacting with Tumi every day also helps me to relate to my own mother and my siblings. I have forgiven them and learned to appreciate them along with their faults and strengths. I now know that they could not hurt me and that they never meant to hurt me in any way. Their world is theirs and mine is mine.

I also needed to acknowledge and forgive my own mother. I now know that I needed to give my mother a place in my life. *Mmala wa kgomo o gola namaneng* (a cow's true colours are reflected in its calf). Everything I hated about being a mother, I had learned through my mother and my background. And everything I needed to do to be a mother to my children, I was learning through my son. It was not fair of me to build my child's world from my mother's world. I have to show my son how to have normal male-female relationships and how to nurture those relationships. I need to teach him how to love and be loved in return without searching for things he didn't know or things that were not meant for him. I am responsible for instilling in him roots and values that will make him a proud man. I want him to know that even when he is allowed to feel pain and fear, there is a power in him to heal the pain and handle the fears but also the power to destroy his life. He needs to be able to make the right choices.

No father ever told me he loved me so I spent my time looking for that feeling of being loved unconditionally. I could not even define what that love meant for me. I grabbed everything and anything that represented my false views of love but I failed because there were no guidelines for how I should be loved and what was acceptable and what was not. I removed myself from relationships and I suffocated in some. I closed myself off from feelings of being loved because I did not know how to share myself without losing myself in the process. I did not know how to find love in myself, so how could I even begin to look for love somewhere else?

Now that I have spent three years alone, looking at life with no pressure to please anyone but myself, I have learned that it was essential to know who I am and what I stand for, or people would hurt me. I have learned to stand up for the truth about myself and not to play the victim any more.

I am now not afraid to choose my battles and to fight them to the end. I am no longer afraid of failure because it is not fatal. I have found courage to be joyful in my own potentials, love, life and relationships. I have found true friendships, courage and love. I have never felt as loved in my life as I am now. After feeling violated, fragile and abandoned as a child, I did not feel worthy of receiving so much love. I grew up with the expectation that receiving anything meant a huge obligation to give back and I would have to be judged and evaluated for what I gave back.

Today I am in touch with myself and my inner being. I now love those long overlooked and undervalued feminine parts of my body and my life that are reflective, collaborative, non-linear, intuitive and creative. I have become happy and content with myself and my experiences. One thing is certain, I am not going to die in pain and in fear; I will die free and peacefully. I am now focusing on everything I still have and all that I will have soon: a future free from pain, fear, anger and resentment. My patience, determination, faith and resilience have got me this far and this is the legacy I want to leave for my children. My single parenting has taught me that life will continue to be unpredictable. I had to start planning a life for Tumi and I without Timothy's input. For the first time I saw the importance of a good support system. I was grateful for my friends and for my mother. I also remembered that my mother had repeatedly told me that dignity and confidence would always help me. I worked hard to maintain my dignity as I dealt with all of my trauma.

I started taking care of myself and the health of my mind and soul. I read a lot to feed my mind with the necessary knowledge and information to assist me in dealing with any situation that comes my way. When I was first diagnosed with endometriosis, I searched for every piece of published information in articles and books to learn more about my condition and how to live with it. When I fell pregnant, I joined a pregnancy chatroom on the Internet for support and information. When I left Timothy, I joined a single parenting support forum on the Internet and understood that I was not alone. I learned about spirituality and the ways of dealing with trauma and finding the courage to heal, and I read biographies of people who had suffered in their lives and managed to triumph.

Through my journey of discovery, I discovered that the same God I had been taught was a punishing God, was actually the One who saw me through all this. I realised all the times that I suffered, I was being humbled – humbled to be equipped to handle the pain, humbled to be conquered by the grace and mercy of the Most High. I was given the power to carry on and with that power I knew how to seek divine intervention, how to pray, how to keep believing and I knew and understood compassion. With the birth of my son, I was given a second chance to live and break free, a chance to surrender completely and to lean on something greater than me.

Perhaps that faith prepared me to face everyone when I came out of the closet about my past. I managed to deal with my ex-pectations and projections about what others would think of me. I now know how to express my emotions – anger, sadness and horror – without fear of embarrassment and rejection. To my doctors, my mother, my son and best friends I have managed to recall all the violent crimes of rape that scarred my identity, along with growing up without a father, the illnesses, and the emotional abuse. I have accepted it all as part of my history and forgave the assailants, no matter how difficult it was; I forgave myself for what I may have done to attract those people in the first place; and grieved over the pain they caused me.

Now I am ready to raise my child with or without a father. In a way, I draw comfort in knowing that despite all my experiences, I have turned out to be someone whom the vast majority of people in my culture envy. I have experienced education and exposure to opportunities for myself as well as opportunities to be generous, to help others and to feel within me that I have more potential, love and strength than I know what to do with.

As part of my spiritual grounding and growth, I have attended workshops and seminars to help me understand myself and my purpose in life. At the end of a recent workshop entitled 'A God who looks like me', a workshop aimed at women who constantly ask the questions 'What is wrong with me? Who will save me?', I made a vow to myself:

> *I am happy being a woman. I know my true goodness. I commit myself to embracing my body as a woman and to feeling beautiful every day. As part of being a woman, I also commit myself to forming and establishing strong and healthy relationships with men, knowing that it is healthy and Godly to be intimate with men. I know there are men who are caring, kind and supportive. I am the daughter of Divine Nature.*

Despite my commitment to growth and self-awareness, life has kept throwing things at me that make me want to quit and question everything that I have come to believe and all that I am still trying to understand. Within a period of three years, I have lost three women who were very dear to me in a subtle and yet profound way. They were my high school friend Tebogo, fourteen months later my cousin Winnifred and after that my sister Angela. No one knew how much these three women meant to

164

me. All the time I have spent and the work I have done in trying to accept and embrace myself as a woman, could not prepare me for the pain and confusion I felt when first Tebogo, then Winnie and finally Angela passed away. I did not cry very loudly or talk to anyone about their deaths. Instead, I slowly retreated into my private space and suffered alone as fear and confusion threatened to take over my life again.

Although I had heard that Tebogo was HIV-positive and ill, I had not seen or spoken to her for three years before her death. The last time I had seen her was at my house in Johannesburg where she was staying while job-hunting. When nothing came of it, she went home after a month and we hardly spoke again. I had noticed when she was with me that I could no longer relate to her in the same way I did back in high school. I was now very well educated, had a well-paid job, a house of my own and I was driving my first car. They were things we had both dreamt of when we were growing up. I was talking about business and career growth and she was talking about single-handedly raising her two children, one of whom was born blind, while unemployed.

When I received news of her death, I could not understand how and why things in Tebogo's life had turned out the way they had. Why? Why? Why? Wasn't she good enough to at least live long enough to enjoy the goodness of this world without pain, to at least retrieve herself from all her disappointments and taste something else? And how was I different? I was reminded that I could have been like Tebogo but I had chosen to run. I might have physically run away but the reality was that I was a single mother, unemployed even after obtaining my degrees and working for successful companies. I felt a void inside me that reminded me I was not who I portrayed myself to be to the outside world. Deep down, I was still living in a state of inner turmoil.

Fourteen months later, I dragged my feet as I walked into the room where my cousin Winnifred was dying. She was like a sister to me. I had learned a lot about being a girl in the house from her. She had taught me how to cook, bake, clean the house and do the laundry. I loved her dearly and yet she might not have known it. I grew up in an environment where sentimental feelings were never shared openly. As long as we got along, that was enough. Who knew what it meant to love someone and give them a special place in your heart? The world around us did not have a clue as to how I felt about her. I never told her, and she never mentioned anything. We didn't really talk much about things other than the household chores and just getting along. Yet, I always watched her closely, observing how she did things and later as I became older and very aware of things, I witnessed the turn of events in her life. She went to college to study for her teacher's diploma. Between the ages of nineteen and thirty-four Winnie had four children, the last of whom died a few months after birth because she, like her mother, was HIV-positive. Though Winnie had worked on a part-time basis, getting 'piece jobs' from the local authorities' offices, she was out of work for very long stretches of time and she never used her teacher's diploma at all. Winnie was constantly smiling and especially bubbly after a couple of drinks. I have always wondered how she could still wear a smile when to me, her life was beset with obstacles and ongoing rough pain and sadness.

On the day that I saw Winnie, three months before her death, I questioned her destiny and how it was going to be possible for her to redeem herself and be vindicated. From when I had been a little girl the concept of vindication had been very important to me. During Religious Education classes at school, we frequently recited from Psalm 24: 'Who may go up the mountain of the Lord? Who can stand in his holy place? He who has a clean hand and a pure heart, who does not lift up his soul to what is false. Who has not sworn deceitfully. He will receive blessings from the Lord, and vindication from the God of his salvation.' Maybe the desire to be vindicated and blessed one day was what kept me going, made it easier for me to move away from my home village. Even in my darkest hour, I always had hope of vindication and I would say the Psalm as a prayer every time I felt lost and weak.

After I visited Winnifred, I swore to myself that I would not die like that. What I saw in that room was something I could not embrace at all. I was determined to stay away from men and from anything in life that represented a danger to my health. I kept postponing going to see Winnie again. I phoned every day to check on her but I was terrified of seeing her. Every time we spoke on the phone she told me she was fine but eventually my mother called to tell me that Winnie had been taken to hospital because she was so weak. She was asking to see me and I promised to come and visit on the Wednesday. At midday on Tuesday, my mother phoned and told me, 'Winnifred passed away an hour ago.'

I went numb. Then I was overwhelmed by an irrational fear that I must be HIV-positive too and I wanted to go to the doctor immediately. I called a friend to tell her how scared I was that my cousin had just died. When she came over to comfort me, all I could say was, 'I am not going to die, I am not going to die, I am not going to die.' I broke out in a rash all over my body and I was unable to describe my feelings or the pain that I was experiencing. I summoned my tears; they came quickly and yet dried up as swiftly as they had appeared. I wanted to mourn the loss of yet another person who I had lived my life trying to be different from, while admiring her courage to continue to smile through it all. I was wracked with guilt. Why wasn't I at her bedside when she died? Was I too scared to see her in her last moments? What would become of me? Should I have been there when she died? What was she going through when she gave up her last breath? Did she think of me as a bad person? Did I abandon her at her time of need? What was I so afraid of?

Before I could find peace or the answers to all these questions, my sister Angela died of colon cancer. She had also never married and left two sons behind. Now all of the women with whom I had identified closely had died.

When Angela died, her loss brought the reality of the loss of Tebogo and Winnie even closer and made my pain all the more overwhelming and hard to comprehend. At a time of death, people experience different things, but I never thought terror and confusion would be my way of mourning the passing of these three women. I became terrified of having known them and terrified of having identified myself with them by my relations with them. My terror was more of how they had lived such painful lives – lives filled with hardship and suffering – and in the end how they had died such tragic deaths. And my confusion related to my own life – something about the lives of Tebogo, Winnifred and Angela and the way they had died made me wonder if it was worth living, wonder and question if it was worth embracing being a woman. How could I continue calling myself a woman when the few things that I knew and had learned about being a woman were shared with these women? I was forced to confront myself as I really was – a confused young woman from a rural village who emigrated to the big city to escape the realities of her own world – but then to acknowledge that my life story did not have to be the same as their life stories.

The passing of Tebogo, Winnifred and Angela terrified me but it also liberated me. Today I am no longer scared to be a woman. I am fighting to be free and to taste happiness, to not die in pain, to at least have happiness and vindication before I pass on. I have realised that I am blessed. I am HIV-negative; I have started my own business and I have found love – self-love, the ability to love and be loved in return. I have found my vindication – a sense of belief, acceptance and trust in myself and the Universe. In spite of all the weakness, all the fear and confusion, the passing of my three sisters made me believe that my choice to be happy and the possibility to demonstrate my freedom does not depend upon the environment I live in, the conditions I find myself in, the location I call my home, my personality or the opportunity to work and be materially wealthy. It depends solely upon my belief and acceptance of myself, and my willingness to take from the world and life all the good that I want and deserve.

May the souls of my sisters rest in peace. I am grateful to have known you and I am blessed by your passing. It has started me on a journey of renewal and acceptance and I am learning how to live my life to the fullest. I have no idea where my journey will lead me. But I continue to walk.

Acknowledgements

This book is written to all the women I know who have tried in many little ways to reach my soul and touch my life. They include my grandmother, my mother, my aunts – Leah, Melida, Rooikie, Martha, Maphari, Sewela – and my schoolteachers who have taught me some of life's lessons. To my cousins – Portia, Ntebaleng, Ermidah, Mokgadi, Audrey and Mohuma – you will always be a part of me as I am of you. To the girls back in Botlokwa – Mathoto, Mosatiwa, Dolly, Mosibudi, Gloria, Moloko, Marara, Francina and my late friend Mokgadi Matsapola – thank you for growing up with me and playing together in our dusty village streets.

Each of the following women has touched me in her own special way: Rethabile Choeu, Nomawethu Maqetuka, Lebohang Ntaka, Ashna Maharaj, Rebecca Motau, Phokeng Mohatlane, Sybil Mokoana, Mapule Modise, Marie-Christine Giraud-Naroskin, Phumla Zazi, Nomathamsanqa Matyeli, Thato Maja, Gwendoline Kgatla, Bernice Letsholo, Siphiwe Msezane, Eunice Railo, Sheila Mashiane, Maria Pooe, Zarina Ismail, Queenie Buthelezi, Thabitha Motau and Korkor Cudjoe. Although some of them are no longer a part of my life, I will always remember their support and love at the time.

My thanks also go to those who have served as my spiritual, psychological and physical support: Reverend Stephanie Clark, Anne Moleko, Dr Bramdev, Dr Kathleen Burns, Dr Modi and Dr Janasch.

170

I also write for all the men who have believed in me: John Godwin, Norman Mathabatha, Edward Mabanna and Gerd Pontow, as well as my two brothers Sylvester and Raymond, and my nephews Pheladi and Godfrey.

To a very special woman in my life, Mathukana Manthata: you know what song to sing for me when I can't sing it myself. Lastly, many thanks to Aubrey, for all the times you have cared.